Penelope Williams continues her journey in the next installment of the Powerhouse Series . . .

At the Edge of the universe, the incursion created by the Kolvat only worsens. The fall of the Academy was only the beginning. The Kolvat were only the beginning. The Witches are losing the war.

A myth from the beginning of the universe provides a glimmer of hope: the Weapons forged by the Witches at the beginning of time could help to drive out the Kolvat, but no one has seen those Weapons in millennia. No one believes they're real anymore.

Back on Earth, Penelope Williams continues her work; work on magic, work on her normal life, work on her freedom. While living with the mother who disowned her, she feels trapped and claustrophobic, no longer allowed to travel where or when she wants. But she is given the task of finding one of the Weapons, rumored to have been hidden in Earth's galaxy for the past several millennia.

A stunning discovery changes everything as a new enemy encroaches on their universe from the outside. The devouring of reality at the Edge of the universe changes the focus of the war. How can they hope to defeat an enemy that can consume reality itself?

Between the rise of this new enemy and her own personal problems, Penelope barely has time to think. She focuses on her quest to find the Weapon and bring an end to the Kolvat. In the process Penelope finds herself trusting an unexpected person. But is that trust misplaced? And will she ultimately regret letting her secrets out?

In this sequel to *Altair*, follow Penelope as she seeks the lost Weapon, tests the limits of her freedom, and adjusts to the changing nature of friendship.

Lucy

L. J. Black

A Powerhouse Novel

Lucy

L. J. Black

For my mother,
who never saw me published

Lucy

I am ashamed
I have forgotten how to do well
and be well
and do right by all
and I am *ashamed*

I am wretched
I feel pain and anguish
and disheartening misery
and depression
and I am *wretched*

I've hurt people
I've caused distress
and disappointment
and disjointed emotions
and I've *hurt people*

I am wicked
I act selfishly
and senselessly
and without consideration
and I am *wicked*

I am not a friend
I do not listen
and do not think
and do not consider
and I am *not a friend*

— Breska Liotson, "I am *not*"

PROLOGUE

"How do we know this will work?"

"We don't. But then again we didn't know the frame would work either."

"Your talent is framing, this is different."

Rather than respond, they lift an appendage and produce a single line of golden power. The energy flows out and forms an arc, whipping around like feisty plasma from a dying star. But still the line holds.

"See? Your talent."

They continue to produce line after line, pausing after each to observe if it holds. The lines connect at the endpoints forming a shape similar to a spherical magnetic field. While simplistic, the shape is effective, and the lines hold together.

"Bring me the matter."

The other takes up the raw matter in their appendage, careful to balance the material. Their form consists of energy and at any moment could convert the matter inadvertently to energy. This small ball of dense material, a fragment of a proto-sphere, balances neatly in the matter-hold they created for it. The other doesn't understand why they need to use matter when energy is the more stable form.

"It is not more stable, just more understood," they answer.

"Why are you trying this?"

There is a pause as they carefully slide the sphere of power around the matter in its holder. The matter glows with the initial energy contact and produces an acoustic reverberation felt in all appendages. The outer shell converts to energy, producing a glow, but then the whole thing stabilizes.

"Because there may be a time when those talented are more matter than energy," they say. "And when that time comes, and they need the raw power of an earlier time, these fragments hidden in matter will be out there to help them."

"Our universe is old already."

"No," they answer. "It only seems old, but it may be very young. And when it is twice the age or fifteen times the age, we might have a very different universe. The Talented might be very different."

Indulgently, the other falls silent, watching as the matter absorbs the power held in the frame. Some time passes, but they do not track it strictly. A turning of the star could have passed in the time it took to imbue the matter with their power. But they wait patiently, energy low as the power moves.

Finally, the matter is laden with their power and they lift it delicately in their careful appendage. The other watches in fascination.

"Now what?" the other asks.

"We let the matter go," they say.

"Go? Where?"

"Anywhere it wants. Into anything it wants."

"What if it becomes part of a planet?"

Nonplussed, they say, "Then the planet will have part of my power. And all subsequent things the planet becomes will have part of my power."

At this place in space where they work, within their favorite star cluster, the matter begins to blow away almost immediately when they hold it up to the stellar wind. Fragments go hither and thither, flying to the far reaches of the system on the unrelenting breeze.

Together the two energy beings watch the fragments go, waiting till the last is lost in the distance.

The other glances around them, gauges the positions of the stars and the relative development of the proto-spheres around them. "Well, that was a way to kill a billion rotations."

They resonate with waves, laughing at their sarcasm. Sarcasm is a new kind of humor, and the two of them enjoy it.

"Shall we find our people?"

"Yes."

Side-by-side they plunge into the depths of space, blazing as photons. Their work is done for now.

PART 1

1

November 20

Penny

Low.

The Earth felt low. The sky low overhead. The ceiling even lower. Emotions low. Energy low. The ground below ready to consume.

My eyes close involuntarily, shutting out the feeling of claustrophobia closing in. The pressing of the room, of the air on my chest, keeping me from breathing. My ribs expand, forcing air in, forcing me to breathe the close atmosphere.

"Penny," Lucy whispers next to me.

My eyes snap open and I glance over at her.

"Are you ok?"

I nod, once, quickly.

We're in the middle of history right now. I haven't heard a word of our teacher's lecture. Not that Mr. Witsorn isn't entertaining. The exact opposite in fact. Since I got back over the summer, my comfort in confined spaces, especially these close classrooms, has only gotten worse. It's been months since I got home.

Lucy knows something is wrong, but she doesn't know why. Doesn't understand that living on Earth again, living in this place on a planet with few to no Witches feels claustrophobic and confining. It's not just that I feel closed in and disconnected from power. It's that I feel alone.

If I were allowed to fully use my power, the feeling might lessen some. My lessons and work are confined to spell matrices and other contained work. My wild power feels hemmed into controlled lines and prescribed working. The freedom I felt on Widdershin, to throw my power in any direction I pleased, is gone. Coldness fills me thinking of the polar cap and the voice of Widdershin.

I remember what Alicia Cole and Harilsen and even Altair have told me. Focus on one small thing. Focus on something real and solid in front of you. I focus on the page of my notes, the words there, the letters sliding into nonsense. The word "civilization" looks like nonsense if you stare at it long enough.

Eventually the class ends, and I pack up my things and head out. Lucy paces me as I leave the building and take a moment under the sun and the free air. School is done for the day. Lucy stands next to me, just outside the building doors, her eyes scanning the crush of students leaving.

My heart is not here. In my mind I see the beautiful landscapes I've left behind. Someday I would find a way to pull those images from my mind and save them somewhere. Velnu and Kaldreesa should be immortalized somehow.

"I'm gonna head to the church," I say to Lucy, excusing myself.

"Do you want my mom to give you a ride?" she asks.

In the back of my mind, I can already feel Ikthiel waiting for me past the trees.

"No, it's ok," I say. "I need to walk."

Lucy gives me a smile. Her mother is waiting along the curb for her. "Don't let your mother get you down," she says, giving me a hug.

I smile back. All I say is, "I'll see you later."

I head away from the school in the direction of my favorite park. Ikthiel will catch up with me so we can walk together through the town. Most people don't see what he really looks like. He also glamours us so we don't appear interesting to look at. People generally leave us alone.

I'm a few blocks away, between school and the park, when the demon falls into step beside me. I smile at him, a genuine if small smile. I always look forward to these visits. Not just his, but all of them. We walk in silence until we come to my usual picnic table. We sit next to each other, facing the water and the bridge.

"What's the news?" I ask.

The demon shrugs, leaning into my shoulder. He hands me what looks like a computer chip the size of a quarter but lighter. "The Kolvat are everywhere it seems," he says. "This is the latest map of their spread as well as some files I could get from Firrl."

"From Firrl?" I say, looking up at the name.

Ikthiel's tiny smile would once have creeped me out, but I know the demon better now. He says, "Among a few correspondences from her and others—Fahum I believe sent one—there is also a significant history database. She gave you what she could on the oldest history of Witches, or Guardians or Protectors or whatever other name."

"Origins?" I study the tiny chip.

"Origins are mostly myth at this point," he says. "The power itself dates back to the earliest days of the universe."

My frustration at not knowing the history of Witches came to a boiling over point when I vented those frustrations to Ikthiel a month ago. Since then, he made it a personal mission to get information to me as often as possible, often without permission, as my lessons still didn't cover this kind of history.

"I did get Firrl to pull some information on the Weapons," he says.

"What weapons?"

Ikthiel pauses, considering how to explain. "Some call them Weapons, others call them Tools or Artifacts," he says. "These are the Tools of the Witches. Wielded by Witches."

"Made by Witches?" I say with sarcasm dripping in my voice.

"I don't know," Ikthiel admits. "Firrl dug into it, but it appears not many Witches really believe in them anymore. They haven't been seen in millennia."

"What made you think of them?"

Ikthiel leans back and looks at me. "I'm not sure," he says. "I might be able to see the future sometimes, but this isn't that. This is more of an instinct or something."

I turn the chip over in my hand, flipping it over and feeling the lightness of it. "Do you think they might help with our current predicament?"

Ikthiel raises and lowers his shoulder. He wraps an arm around my shoulders and squeezes them. I lean into the odd sideways hug. "I'm just afraid," he whispers. Ikthiel never admits to fear, so I feel like this is genuine. And I can feel in him the strain of fear underneath his cool exterior.

I wrap my arm around his waist and say, "I'm afraid too."

The image of the Kolvat sinking to the north pole of Widdershin comes unsummoned to my mind. Fear clenches my heart at the thought.

"I'm sure there's something we can do," he says. "I just haven't found it yet."

"What about your demon friends," I ask, the thought suddenly coming to me. "What do they say?"

"Not much," he admits. "Only that the Kolvat weakening the Witches has to be good for all demons. They're too short-sighted. Even Disperao."

A trill of fear plays through Ikthiel as he mentions the space-time demon. A couple months ago he had described his demon friends to me. I had given him a hard time because I knew so little about him. He knows so much about me. So, he started telling me things. We hadn't gotten too personal yet, but slowly he was opening up. The one thing he did tell me is how much Disperao scares him.

I sigh. "I guess I should get going."

Ikthiel nods and gets up from the table. He gives me a hand getting up and carrying my extra books. It's been a rough week for homework, but nothing, not even college on Earth, will ever compare to exam week at the Academy.

Together we get up and head to the church. I often drag my feet, but I don't really hate it. This time of year, heading towards Thanksgiving, the church is starting to get into the holiday spirit. There's something about that uplifting feeling that is starting to get to me.

I don't think I really believe in religion anymore, not in that way anyway. But I've learned there is a higher power than what is in our everyday grasp. On some level I'm still angry about it. I'm angry about being sent to the abusive camp back when I was a new Witch. I'm angry that religion is why my father tried to beat the power out of me. But I don't think I'm angry at God. I think I'm angry at people who misinterpret what they believe God wants them to think.

"You ok?" Ikthiel asks, pulling me out of my thoughts.

I smile up at him. "I don't know," I say honestly. The trauma of my past still creeps up on me.

"You were going down the past," he says. He takes my hand in his, my mind feeling his seeping in. He is worried. About me, about my situation, about everything.

I squeeze his hand. "I'm not sure what to think anymore." He squeezes my hand back. He doesn't say anything, but he doesn't have to. I can read him now so much better than before. Really I just feel brave enough to.

We get within a block or so of the church and I let go of his hand. I stop and turn to him, looking into his dark eyes. "I can't stay here forever," is all I can think to say.

"I know," he says. "I have a treat for you, when you're ready to go offworld. Maybe a Christmas or a birthday present."

My eyebrows go up. He isn't the kind of person who does presents. "Anytime," I say.

"After the holidays then," he says. He pulls me into a hug. "I'll be back in a couple weeks. I've got a commission a ways away."

He never says where. I prefer it that way.

I hug him back and then pull away. "I'll see you later."

I head toward the church. I feel Ikthiel disappear behind me.

2

November 20

Lucy

The bubbling of the fish tank provides gentle background noise to doing homework. No matter how much work I do, there never seems to be enough time to get through it all. Especially at this point in high school when grades are starting to matter.

The history lecture today can't keep my mind on things. I keep thinking about how Penny hasn't been the same since she got back. I expected her to be off a bit, having been gone so long. But I don't think I expected her to be this different. She is closed off in ways I didn't expect. We used to talk about things, but I get the feeling she is holding back.

A knock on the door jogs me out of my thoughts. Bryce pokes his head in. I smile up at him and he comes in, shutting the door gently behind me. My mother must have let him in.

"How's it going?" he asks, plopping down on my bed and gesturing at the history textbook I'm ignoring.

"Not well," I admit. "I can't keep my mind on things."

"What's bothering you?" he asks.

Since we started dating, he has done nothing but show me courtesy and respect. I enjoy the company with him because he is so honest with me. In return I am honest with him.

"It's Penny," I explain. "She's changed."

"How so?"

I tilt my head thinking. I'm not sure how to explain it to him. "You didn't really know her before," I say, not asking because I know it's the truth. "She went through a lot with her family."

Bryce's eyebrows knit together. "You never really told me about that, but I've heard rumors."

"Yeah, and I'm sure you saw her broken arm."

"Was that from her family?" he asks, incredulous.

"No," I answer with knit eyebrows, "she said it was from a fall. Which I believe, but that broken arm certainly started rumors."

Bryce just shakes his head. "My mother never said much about her meetings with Penny," he says. "I know she was worried about her though."

We all were, I think.

"Either way," I say, "she just feels more closed off and distant since she got back. Like she went through something she doesn't want to talk about. I shudder to think what could have happened to her at that boarding school."

Bryce reaches out and squeezes my hand. I smile at him wanly. Anxiety is not my style. I know he is concerned about how I'm knotting herself up in a ball over this. But I can't quite let it go.

"Do you want to take a walk? Get your mind off of it?"

The sigh that escapes me says more than my words do. I look hopelessly at the history texts in front of me and shake my head.

"You can study later," Bryce says teasingly. He knows how important my studies are to me.

The best I can do is let go and get my mind off things. So I finally nod and shut my textbook and put my shoes on. And we walk downstairs.

"Hey mom, we're going for a walk."

"Ok, be careful," she says absently with a wave. She is too engrossed in her work at the moment to pay much attention.

We head out the door and down the street, hand in hand as we have been for months now. I think the advent of Bryce surprised me the most while Penny was gone. I felt really lonely with my best friend gone. And it hasn't gotten much better since she's been back, what with her mom keeping her isolated. But it can't last forever, especially if Penny is back for good.

"Do you want to walk by there?" Bryce asks suddenly. He gives my hand a squeeze as if he had been reading my mind this whole time.

"Yeah, I'd like to," I say. And we take the next turn onto Penny's street and head down the block. It's four in the afternoon so maybe she'll be home, or maybe she'll still be at that awful church with her mom. But sure enough the driveway is empty and her house is probably empty as well. We still walk down the street and go up to the front door and knock.

After a few minutes of waiting and having rung the doorbell twice, we both shrug and head back down the street. There doesn't seem to be any point in waiting. I know they won't be home for a bit.

"What are your Thanksgiving plans?" Bryce asks.

It will be Thanksgiving this week and I hadn't really thought about it. "The usual I guess," I say. "My parents always do the big meal at lunch. Then we have pie for dinner."

"My parents do dinner," he says. "Can I come over for lunch?"

I look at him, cooly assessing him in a way I hadn't in a while. I like Bryce, that's the easy part. The question is how much do I like him. Do I like him enough to invite him over for a holiday meal with my parents? I wish I could ask Penny. She hasn't been around enough, but this is the exact kind of thing I would bounce off her.

She would probably tell me I'm being silly and overthinking. She would probably tell me that I should just let go and go with it.

"I'll check with my parents," I say. I do have to get permission. "Your family wouldn't mind?"

"Not at all," he says confidently. "Like I said we have our big meal at night. You could come if you want. I can check, but I'm sure they'd be fine with it."

"I'll ask my parents," I say quickly. The idea of breaking with my routine unsettles me. Somehow, even though I know I'm being ridiculous, this feels like one of those changes that comes with adulthood. Visiting the boyfriend's family for Thanksgiving feels like a rite of passage somehow.

Bryce takes my hand as we walk towards my house. The silence between us feels companionable. My mind relaxes and I let go of my trepidations about the holiday. With Bryce's hand in mine, it doesn't feel like a big deal. It feels natural.

"Why don't we walk to the church and see if Penny is there,"

Bryce suggests suddenly. I'm not sure where the idea comes from but I'm grateful he has had it. The church is not far, so we can walk there.

"You don't mind?"

"Of course not."

We turn around and head toward the main road. The church is about a quarter mile down from there. We take our time in the heat of the afternoon. The church comes into sight, and we cross the grass parking lot. I pull on the front door only to find it locked.

"The office must be open," Bryce suggests.

He leads me down the church steps and around the building. We head to the back section where the Sunday school and the administrative offices are. The door marked "Main Office" has its blinds open and we can see Penny's mom sitting behind a desk.

Bryce opens the door for me and I step through.

"Hi, Mrs. Williams," I say. Belatedly I remember she is now divorced and might not want to be called Mrs. Williams.

"Hello Lucy," she says. "Bryce. What can I do for you two?"

"Is Penny here?" I ask.

Mrs. Williams's brow furrows but she answers, "She's in the back working on homework."

"Can we go see her?"

She stares at us for a moment. Then she lets out a deep sigh and says, "I guess so. Don't distract her for too long."

I can't contain the smile. I genuinely thought she would say no. I genuinely thought I would never get her approval. And this isn't approval, but it is one step closer.

Bryce and I head to the second part of the office where the filing cabinets keep track of the school and all the baptismal and other church records. There, at the table in the middle of the room, Penny sits with pages and books spread out in front of her. Her clothes are as strange as they have been since she got back. Her mom picks them out, she had admitted to me. Today she is wearing a button up blouse that hangs loosely on her and a denim skirt that goes to her knees. The denim is a concession from her mother. It gives Penny something of a normal appearance at school. Her shoes are the only thing that I think Penny really picks out. Today they are grey Van's.

"Does mom know you're back here?" she asks. Compulsively

Penny pulls her hair tie out to redo her ponytail.

"She sent us back."

The surprise registers on Penny's face.

"She said not to distract you too long," I add.

Penny smiles. "I finished thirty minutes ago. I've been reviewing."

Bryce pulls out a chair and sits down. I take one next to him, looking around the room.

"What are your Thanksgiving plans?" Bryce asks Penny.

She shrugs. "I'm not sure," she says. "The usual I think. Lunch at one or something."

"Why don't you ask your mom if you can come over to my house for late dinner?" Bryce asks. "Penny is coming."

Even though that isn't set in stone yet, I nod and agree that I'm coming. I don't want to deter her with uncertainty.

"I can ask," she says. The lack of enthusiasm says she isn't hopeful that her mom will say yes. I would say her estimate of her odds is accurate. Secretly I hope she does come. It'll make me going to Bryce's house less real. I wonder if that's why he invited her.

A sudden thought crosses my mind. I push back the smile at my brilliance. I think for a moment and then suggest, "Why don't you come to my house and we can ride over together?"

"I could do that," Penny says. A tiny smile crosses her face. "I'll ask but no promises."

I nod at her words.

"We should go before your mom gets mad," Bryce says.

He gets up from the table and helps me out of my chair. For a moment I see a flicker of knowing on Penny's face.

"Thanks for stopping by," she says. Her voice is as lifeless as it usually is, but the words are sincere. I head out of the back room and pass Mrs. Williams wondering briefly how much she overheard.

Outside we walk the length of the church in silence and it's only when we turn down the main street that Bryce finally speaks.

"Why did you invite her to your house?"

I grin at my brilliant idea again. "I'm gonna loan her some clothes for dinner. I'm gonna give her one night where she's back to her normal self."

Bryce puts his arm around my shoulders and says, "I love it."

I smile to myself. I know that's not what he means. I know he loves me though we haven't said it to each other. I keep my thoughts to myself as we walk down the street and back to our neighborhood.

Later. We'll say it to each other later.

3

November 26

Penny

I stand in the kitchen staring down my mother. I don't want to cause more problems than I already had, but I wasn't taking no for an answer on this.

She stands across her counter from me, looking disapprovingly at my suggestion. I want to see Lucy and go with her to Bryce's house for Thanksgiving.

"I don't want you associating with them." Her words make no sense.

I shake my head. "Why?" I ask. "They're both human. They're not Witches or demons or aliens. They're ordinary humans. You have no reason to dislike them."

My mother clenches her jaw. "I don't like either of their families' beliefs. And you can't argue with that. Plus you are staying in my house. You will abide by my rules."

I can't stand this. Not anymore. I'm done. I hate to be like this and to pull this card, but I'm going to.

"Mom, you can't keep me here. One message and there will be a demon in your kitchen. One message and there will be more Witches in this house than you know what to do with." I pause and gauge her reaction. She is alarmed. "I don't want to be like that, but I've done more than enough to accommodate what you want. I'm not going to give up my friends the way I've given up everything else about my identity to keep from offending you."

My mother looks like she wants to smack me for being impertinent. After what my father did, I know she won't lay so much as a finger on me. She hasn't touched me once since I got back.

Her hands clench and unclench. I can feel the anger. I don't care. I'm angry too. I hate living here, wearing the clothes she picks, avoiding using my magic. I hate all of this.

"I'm going," I say with finality.

"Fine," she relents. "Be back by nine."

Then she storms out of the kitchen and I'm left stunned that I even got that minor assent. I don't know what to do so I just stand there for a few minutes staring into space. Then I snap out of it. A bubble of joy wells up inside me for the first time in a long time. I almost don't recognize the feeling at first. The smile on my face feels genuine and I hold back the giggle inside me. I had forgotten what joy feels like. Even out in the universe I hadn't felt more than mildly happy. It took a win like this to make me smile.

I shake off my thoughts. It's getting late. Lucy had asked me to come to her place early before going to dinner. I should leave now so my mother doesn't have time to change her mind. I grab my keys and my phone and head out the front door.

Lucy's house is only a couple blocks from me, the door a cheerful blue. I knock on the door and wait for an answer. It's Lucy's mother who opens the door.

"Hi, Mrs. St. John," I say.

"Penny, come on in. Lucy is upstairs waiting for you."

"Thank you." I walk in and Mrs. St. John shuts the door behind me.

"I'm glad your mother is letting you go to Thanksgiving dinner with Lucy and Bryce," she says suddenly.

I'm not sure what to say, so I just say, "Me too," and head up the stairs to Lucy's room.

Upstairs I head down the hallway to the third door which is cracked open about an inch. "I just hope she likes it," a voice I recognize Lucy's filters through the door. I knock once and crack the door open.

Inside her room, I find Lucy standing behind her bed with several pieces of clothes carefully laid out on the bedspread. At the foot of the bed, several pairs of her shoes take up space. Bryce stands off to one side of the room.

"What's going on?" I ask tentatively.

"Surprise!" Lucy says. "I wanted to give you a night of normalcy, so I'm lending you some of my clothes."

My jaw drops. I am dressed as my mother dresses me in conservative clothing consisting of a button-down blouse and a knee-length skirt.

"Do you mean it?" I ask. I haven't felt like myself since I started wearing these clothes and getting a night to feel like me would be a blessing.

"I mean it," Lucy says, coming around the bed to give me a hug. For a moment I don't feel anything but surprise. Then in the arms of Lucy's embrace I feel the tears start. I don't cry much since everything happened with my family, but this got to me. This is enough to reach me in my coldness.

"Thank you," I croak out in between the tears and the sobs. I'm embarrassed at how much I want to cry over this and I'm cringing that I'm doing it in front of Bryce.

"Anything, anytime," Lucy says, giving me one last squeeze before pulling away. "Now pick something and get changed. We need to get going."

I take a step forward and survey her clothes. I pull a pair of jeans out thinking about the last time I wore them—the day I left Earth for the Academy. It will bring me back there for sure. And there on top of the pile of shirts is a top Lucy knows I love. It's one of her favorites, but she's loaned it to me before. It's a black tank with crochet lace along the neckline. I pull it from the pile and hug it close.

"How did I know?" Lucy says teasingly.

I grin at her, my second genuine smile of the day. I head for the bathroom. There, behind a shut door, I look in the mirror and see a happy version of myself for the first time in years. It won't last—my depression is not going to go away because of one small gesture like this. But today, of all days, I will enjoy it until I have to go home later. I wipe the tears from my eyes and change my clothes.

When I rejoin Lucy and Bryce in her bedroom, she is putting away the extra clothes and Bryce is standing awkwardly, holding shoes. Lucy looks up and smiles at me. "You look great," she says. "What shoes do you want to wear?"

My feet are about a half size smaller than hers, but I can make it work with the right pair of shoes. I pull a pair of black dressy sandals from Bryce's arms and slip them on. They're the right style, and they should stay on my feet at least. I wouldn't be running any marathons in them, but they would work.

"We should get going," Bryce says. "Mom likes to have hors d'oeuvres before we eat a big meal, I don't know why."

"Sounds good to me."

"Let's go," Lucy says. She takes the shoes from Bryce and unceremoniously flings them into her closet. She then leads me and Bryce out of the bedroom.

"Bye, Mom!" Lucy calls as we all head out the front door. We'll be walking around the block to Bryce's house.

"Have fun!" Lucy's mom calls absently from the living room. She and Lucy's father are on the couch watching some of the evening Thanksgiving programming. The normalcy of it strikes me for a moment. But I don't have a second to dwell on it.

We head down the street and go a few blocks over to Bryce's street. Luckily the weather is more temperate than it has been. The walk taking twenty minutes isn't unbearable. We walk up to Bryce's house, and he lets us in.

"There you are!" his mother calls from the kitchen. She is drying a glass with a checkered towel, and the image of this woman doing something so normal strikes me as comforting. For a moment, goosebumps run up my neck. But then it passes, and I dismiss it as ASMR.

"Come in!" Bryce's mother says, waving us inside the house. Bryce shuts the door behind us. His mother makes eye contact with me as she asks, "How are you doing, Penny?"

I know she knew about the abuse my family put me through, if not explicitly then she suspected it. I would never tell anyone about what happened with my father, though. And no one needs to know how harsh my mother still is with me. So all I say is, "I'm doing fine."

"Glad to hear it," she says.

I flash back for a moment to when she was my principal and when she asked me if I was safe. And I wonder how different it would have been if I had just trusted an adult and told the truth that I didn't feel safe. But you can't change the past. And I don't feel the need to try.

"Come sit down everyone," she continues. "We have hors d'oeuvres ready to munch on while the turkey is resting."

I take a seat, running my hands along the soft fabric of Lucy's jeans. It feels odd to be dressed so normally. I decide at that moment to forget my home life problems. And to forget about being a Witch cut off from all her people. So I let go and let myself be here in this place where everyone is kind and welcoming and accepting of me.

I reach for a tiny quiche and savor the bite.

4

January 20

Penny

Christmas is over. I feel like it never really happened, but that's just my morbid sense of reality right now. My Christmas hasn't felt normal since before I became a Witch, since I felt like the holiday was something to be excited over.

This year Mom didn't even try. Sure, she put up a tree, dove into the celebrations at the church, and even did a dinner. But she didn't pretend it was some family holiday that brought people together. In a way this was the best Christmas I had had since I was ten. In another sense it was the saddest.

Lucy and her family gave me presents. Lucy has finally been allowed over to my house after I put my foot down with my mother. It took long enough, but now that she's allowed over, she comes over in the evening almost every day to cheer me up. And Bryce has started coming over too. The two of them got together while I was gone and apparently have been inseparable since. I don't mind. Bryce has always been nice to me.

My birthday is coming up, but I have low expectations for that as well. I know I'll be spending time with Lucy at the beach, but other than that I'm not sure what's going to happen. Which is why it took me by surprise when Ikthiel showed up in my bedroom five days before my birthday.

"I want to take you somewhere special," he says. The words at

23

one point would have scared me. Why would a demon want to take me anywhere? Would I be safe there? But we are friends now. Closer friends than anyone else in my life, even Lucy.

"Where are we going?"

"It's a surprise." Again, this might have scared me in the past, but now I feel safe with Ikthiel. I will likely always feel safe with him.

"Ok," I assent after a pause. "When do you want to go?"

"Now," he says.

I open my bedroom door and listen. It is late, after eight in the evening. My mother is downstairs watching tv. I softly shut my door and turn back to Ikthiel.

"We have to be back before ten," I say. I figure we have two hours before she comes up to bed and checks on me.

"I can make that happen," he says. He extends his clawed hand to me. I take it without flinching even a little.

My vision goes dark.

I blink and find myself in a strange place. Darkness fills the space but incompletely, as if shadow shrouds the whole area. Nothing but unyielding rock fills my view, and even that tests the eye, uncomfortable as it is to look at. My eye meets no horizon. Above us, no sky. Just rock and even that I feel is an illusion. I breathe, not with my natural lungs or the portable atmosphere, but with the demonic trick Ikthiel taught me. Without it I would not breathe at all. The stillness in the air, mimicking the shadow of the light, feels both hostile and welcoming. Somehow, I feel we have disturbed a long slumber.

The taint of old magic, older than I have ever felt before, sizzles in the air just out of reach. The magic predates even that in the oldest, deepest parts of Widdershin. Even in the depths of Firrl's research lab, that magic would be infantile compared to this.

"Where are we?" I whisper to Ikthiel. I wince at the sound. My voice is flattened in the unnatural atmosphere.

He answers with his mind, *Most Witches have forgotten this place exists. Your kind forgets its own history.*

The mantra is familiar. For years many have lamented to me the lack of understanding of our past. I still know nothing of early Witches, even of those on Earth.

Ikthiel squeezes my hand, and I squeeze his back. I feel small and childlike here, a feeling I have not experienced in a long time. Through the contact, in the back of Ikthiel's mind, I sense that he feels the same: young and frightened.

He leads me forward, toward a nondescript rock face that could be any other rock face here. Only when we draw near to it do I feel the subtle heat emanating from deep within. A touch of the power is embedded here, definitively originating from a Witch and not a demon or other creature. So quietly it tries to hide, concealing itself as well it can.

Place your hand on the rock, Ikthiel instructs silently.

I look at him, fear flaring in me. Our gazes meet and I feel the reassurance that it is no illusion, it will not harm me, I will be safe.

I reach forward and my hand goes through the rock.

Together we step through the solid surface, rock that no longer wishes to be solid and has chosen not to be. Together we feel the tickling of unrepentant but yielding stone. Deeper we walk into it until I feel we must be going so deep we might never come out. And then, just when my lungs begin to feel the pressure and my mind begins to panic, the way is clear. The rock retreats. We enter a cavern of sorts, though a small one at best.

The space barely exceeds that of my bedroom back on Earth. The moment we push through, the rock solidifies behind us, and I find myself leaning on it, gaining distance from what is here in the middle. The heat from the power burns my face and hands, no doubt leaving a mild burn. Even blinking multiple times cannot completely adjust my eyes.

Hanging in the center of the cavern, maybe a few feet off the ground, a simple spell matrix buzzes with power and manifest strength the likes of which I have never seen. The matrix feels as old as time itself. But the power has not degraded like so many others. Even simple Witch lights require refueling regularly. This has been going strong since it was placed here.

A single ring makes up the matrix, but not a clean one like mine. It is not so defined nor so dim. It is a blazing ring of uncontrolled lighting that burns the eyes to look at. The circle appears as if it has been drawn by a child, wildly approximating what a circle should look like but brazenly not caring about the accuracy. Whoever put this here had not been practiced at spell matrices.

That is because this was placed by the first Witch to use spell matrices, Ikthiel whispers in my mind. *They are long gone now, but this lives on somehow.*

I feel the incredulity soften my features from fear to awe. I take half a step forward, Ikthiel moving with me.

In that movement the matrix flares up and recognizes us in earnest. A tendril of power shoots out a stepped leader of intention, making its way to both of us without either of us being able to react. The power touches my heart. I look down at it, feeling the power testing the Spark still there within my heart. One glance at Ikthiel and I see it doing the same. For some reason the power has not recoiled from him as most Witches would.

He finally says the thing I have known for years, known intuitively, but never heard him admit. *I was a Witch once.*

I had heard many voices, belonging to planets and demons and realms and even the power within. I had not heard a matrix have a voice before, perhaps because they did not live long enough to develop one. This matrix had. And it did not speak with words; it spoke in ways I could not describe. I am not sure if it was through our shared power that it communicated, but it did speak.

In my memory, a memory not mine but belonging to the matrix, I saw the Witch who laid the power here. The Witch who appeared to the matrix only as a bright Spark and a form made solely of energy. They were as different from me as Namawh is from any human. And yet they would be so different from Namawh, an earlier energy being, that even Namawh's little bit of matter would be preposterous to them.

And in that Spark, I see a reflection of my own Spark. And a reflection of Ikthiel's unused Spark. And for that moment they all seem the same.

But they are.

Maybe they weren't words. Not those words exactly. The truth is there. The truth in the power. That our power, the power behind the Sparks and the demons and the other creatures I have met and maybe even the Kolvat: it's all the same. That somehow the multiverse of creatures all have the same power. I'm not sure why it's significant, but it feels like a revelation that will one day turn the tide.

Then the spell matrix lurches forward and my mind goes

elsewhere.

A tendril of power comes out and touches my wrist and the communicator there. The power imbued in the communicator reacts to the touch and becomes more real. As if the spell within it reacted to this oldest of spell matrices by absorbing some of its old true power. As if something like that could change and be made anew.

Then a tendril reaches for my heart and my Spark again. I don't know what to make of it when it touches me and goes through my skin like my body doesn't matter. Maybe it doesn't. But I feel the contact with my Spark, the direct alignment of the spell matrix with myself. And I suddenly understand in ways I never thought I could.

I know in that moment it will take me half a lifetime to process and understand what I learned from the spell matrix. But I also know that a spell matrix can be made in ways I had never imagined. I know if I can deepen my understanding of this ancient creature, then I might be able to help all the Witches and not just the ones that need my power.

The matrix retreats. It settles down, not going out but clearly satisfied and going dormant again. Ikthiel takes my hand again and together we back through the stone and out again.

The flat unusual space meets us, and I truly do not understand why the spell is here in this odd pocket of reality.

It chooses to be here, Ikthiel says.

Chooses to be a hermit, to live in isolation in this space created for it or that it created.

I don't know, the demon admits. *I don't know who or what created the space.*

I look around one more time, but I am ready to leave this place. I am ready to return to the familiarity of home. I may not feel entirely safe there, but I am ready for something entirely mundane after this experience.

Ikthiel lets go of my hand and pulls me into a hug. He holds me like that as we teleport back to my bedroom. I breathe the familiar air again.

5

January 23

Penny

The weather is cold for Georgia. It doesn't matter though. For my birthday, Lucy wanted to take me to the beach. And I couldn't think of any reason why not. So, I was getting ready to go when the doorbell rang. I could hear my mother answer it and didn't think anything of it till she called my name.

"Lucy!"

I zip up my duffel bag and take it downstairs with me. I round the corner of the staircase and face the door.

"Firrl!"

I drop my bag and run to the giant fish woman who is currently in human form. There's no mistaking who she is though. She still somehow looks like herself even as a human. I throw my arms around the tall woman, and she does the same, lifting me off my feet to embrace me.

"Mom, this is Firrl," I say by way of introduction when she puts me down.

"Hello," is all my mom can think to say.

Firrl extends a hand in a gesture she probably only just learned. My mother shakes her hand warily. "Nice to meet you," Firrl says.

"Are you staying long?" I ask. Firrl is one of the Witches who has maintained the most contact with me. I hear from her on a regular basis. She helped me work through some of the feelings of letdown I had after my Spark did not get used.

"As long as you want," Firrl says. "I'm here for your birthday."

For a moment I can't say anything. Having another Witch around me is a privilege these days. Then the reality settles down and I say, "You should come to the beach with us."

Her eyes get so big I'm almost concerned for a moment. "Are you sure? Can I?"

"Let me just text Lucy to let her know."

I tap my wrist communicator, currently disguised as a smart watch, and send a message to Lucy. Knowing her I wouldn't need to wait long for the response. And just like that I get a message from her saying "Sure!"

"She says you should come," I answer. For the first time in a long time, I feel a bubble of optimism well up inside me. I feel happiness and gratitude at being in the presence of another Witch, not a demon, not someone who knows about Witches, a full-blooded power-holding Witch. I haven't felt that since I left the ship to come back to Earth. The relief is extreme.

Then I turn to my mother who is frowning in disapproval. She makes eye contact with me, and I feel like she has dumped a bucket of ice water over my head. The attempt at a smile fades. The anger wells up inside me again. I think Firrl senses it because she reaches out and gently touches my arm. I smile wanly at her. She doesn't say anything, silently or aloud. Neither do I.

"We should get going," is all I can think to say after a pause.

"Hold on."

The words from my mother's mouth sound loaded with misgiving.

I shoulder my duffel bag and turn back to her. "What?"

"Don't take that tone with me," she says warningly. I narrow my eyes at her. "I mean it. I said you could go. I never said anything about any friends of yours from that school."

I clench my jaw. "No, but then again, I didn't agree to completely give up my friends either." I immediately regret saying it, but it is the truth. And she needs to back off.

Firrl's hand comes down on my shoulder, a gentle reminder to take a breath. Which I do. But it never helps to breathe these days. My anxiety and depression are beyond the strength of a good deep breath.

My mother bristles at my words, her eyes darting from me to Firrl and back again. For a moment I think she is going to argue. She opens and closes her mouth several times. Then she seems to shake it off and simply says, "Fine. Just be back on time."

"We will," Firrl says, before I can say something regrettable. My anger simmers just below the surface, waiting to rear its ugly head. Sometimes I forget everything I have learned to control it. Sometimes I just want to lose control.

Firrl steers me out of the house. My mother shuts the door behind us. Together the fish person and I begin the walk to Lucy's house where I know they're waiting for us.

Firrl doesn't say anything for a while, but as we turn the corner onto Lucy's street she says, "Your mother is difficult."

"She's better than she used to be," I grumble. "But you are correct. She is difficult."

"Is she treating you well?"

"Not well. But I will say she is better than she was." That is the truth. As difficult and overbearing as my mother could be, she didn't turn me away when I needed a place to live. And though she is strict with her rules and keeping up appearances while I live with her, she doesn't restrict me as much as she could. I shake off the disgusted feeling I have from defending her mentally and keep walking.

I lead Firrl up to Lucy's door and knock. Lucy herself answers it.

"Hey, Luce," I say. "This is Firrl from school."

Lucy lights up and extends a hand to Firrl. The fish woman shakes it in bemusement. "Nice to meet one of Penny's friends from school!"

"I'm just glad I got the time to visit," Firrl says.

"Come on in!" Lucy says, ushering us inside.

In the living room Bryce stands up to greet us. He gives me a hug and shakes Firrl's hand as well. "Nice to meet you," he says genially.

It always surprises me how at ease both Lucy and Bryce are around new people. Especially someone as odd as Firrl.

"What grade are you?" Lucy asks Firrl.

"I actually graduated," Firrl says, which is the truth though they don't know she graduated quite a long time ago.

"Oh, ok," Lucy says. "I thought you might be older. You're so tall!"

Firrl laughs and says, "It runs in the family." Which is probably true, but they don't know how different Firrl's family is.

"Yeah," Firrl says. "Penny and I met on a research project at school."

"What kind of research?" Lucy asks, immediately interested.

"Genetics," is all Firrl answers. There's no way to explain or spin what kind of genetics and what kind of tracking they are doing. As far as I know, they had set up another lab on another planet, somewhere central to the galaxy that is out of the way enough not to be disturbed by Witches going about their work. I have been curious to see the lab for quite some time, but I doubt I will be able to see it anytime soon.

Lucy's mother comes into the room just then, giving us a reprieve from all the questions. The introductions are made again, and Mrs. St. John lets us know that they are ready to leave if everyone wants to get in the SUV.

Firrl squeezes into the back row of the SUV along with me and Lucy. Mr. St. John wouldn't be joining us, so Bryce sat up front. It was a tight squeeze, but we made it work. I sat wedged between my childhood best friend and the only friend who wasn't obligated to work with me at the Academy. Something felt right about this. As we drove the half hour to Jekyll Island, I sat back in my seat, watching as Firrl marveled at the landscape and Lucy kept herself busy on her phone.

We turn the last corner to the beach parking on Jekyll Island, and Lucy's mom parks the SUV. One by one we pile out of the car and head towards the sound of water.

Firrl's reaction is everything. The sheer look of delight on her face at the wide expanse of water in front of her brings happiness to my soul. I didn't know I could still feel this way at someone else's joy.

We take off our sandals and walk barefoot on the sand, feeling the grains scrubbing clean the last dregs of the city. I feel myself calming in the presence of the great ocean. This is why I always seek out water to watch and be near. I find the proximity to be calming.

"Wow," Firrl whispers. "It's been too long."

"How long has it been?" I whisper back.

"Since before Widdershin," she answers. I know she never had time to swim on Widdershin. I know she doesn't have much time to herself now. And there's no telling whether she lives near enough to an ocean to go swimming.

"Do you miss the planet?"

"Do you?" she asks back.

The answer to both questions is of course yes. There's nothing we can do. The final cries of Widdershin still haunt my dreams. Me, the world-breaker. Me, the planet-killer. The responsibility of the planet's death rests squarely on my shoulders.

"No, it doesn't," Firrl whispers. "The Kolvat killed the planet long before you took its life."

I shake my head, trying to hold back tears and the feeling of failure. "I just wish I could have saved it. I wish the planet didn't have to die."

Firrl rests her hand on my shoulder, giving it a gentle squeeze of solidarity. She says words of comfort, but I don't hear them. I don't hear the logic in knowing I'm not responsible. I just hear my own pain.

Lucy walks past us to the water, her smiling face breaking my reverie. "C'mon! Let's get in the water!"

And just like that the spell is broken, and I am in the present again instead of back on that ice sheet on Widdershin.

"Let's go," Firrl says chasing after Lucy. I smile to myself, a somewhat genuine smile, and follow my friends. Bryce is not far behind us.

When we get to the water's edge, we pause. It's chilly today. I delicately put my toes in the water and the frigidity almost makes me draw back. Lucy takes my hand on one side, Firrl takes the other hand, and Bryce takes Lucy's free hand. We grin at each other and run headlong into the surf. Sometimes the only way to get over something is to dive straight in.

6

January 25

Penny

The day of my birthday I wake up with a sense of optimism I hadn't felt in a long time. I don't know why, but I felt like something good is going to happen.

The feeling lasts the whole day at school. Lucy brought me a cupcake her mom had made for me. She smuggled a candle and a lighter into school and we almost got in trouble before I blew it out. It felt normal and good to just do something slightly rebellious. I felt like a normal teenager for once.

Fifteen feels old to me. Fifteen feels like I've spent so much of my life already. I know it's just an artifact of being through so much at my age, but I feel the burden anyway. All the trauma I suffered two years ago at my father's hands comes back on days like this. So, I sat in my last class of the day, staring out the window as usual, and thinking hard about what my life was going to look like after I leave Earth again.

Lucy catches up with me after class. She doesn't say anything at first but stops me outside the front doors of the school. She reaches in her backpack and hands me a small box wrapped in silver paper.

"Happy Birthday," she says. "I didn't get to give it to you at lunch because I left it in my locker."

I smile and take the box from her. "Should I open it now?" I ask.

She nods enthusiastically.

I carefully peel back the paper revealing a brown box. I slide the lid off and inside is a jewelry box. Inside the jewelry box is a silver necklace with a tiny pair of fish on it forming a symbol like a yin and yang.

"Koi fish," she explains. "One for each of us."

I can't help but smile. A fish necklace is so exactly what she would get me. She takes the box from me as I pull the necklace out of the case. I put it on immediately.

"I know you don't really wear jewelry," she says, "but I figured this could a special thing you have."

I look down at the koi fish and say, "Thank you. I really mean it." I give her a hug and take the box back from her. She tosses the wrapping paper in a convenient trash can near the school entrance.

"Can I come by later?" she asks.

"I'll ask my mom, but I'd like that." Even though we just went to the beach together, having company on my birthday would be nice.

Lucy's mom drives up to the school in her SUV. She waves at us and we both wave back.

"Text me when you know," she says as she heads to the car. "Do you want a ride?" she asks.

I shake my head. It's really not a far walk, and I want to keep thinking. "See you later," I say, willing that to be true.

I head to the church like usual. My mind goes back to my thoughts of a life off Earth. I want to be out there among the stars. I think once your worldview opens up to incorporate other solar systems, it's hard to go back to being confined on one planet. It's hard to go back to normal. My normal is now out there.

Ikthiel crosses my mind as I think about all the places I could go and people I could live with. My preference for his company still puts people off, but I honestly don't care. If I feel safe around him, then whose business is it anyway? No one's. I care about him, and that's enough for me.

The afternoon is not overly warm for once, so I am not sweating as I walk up to the office door. As I come through the door, I know something is up.

"There you are," my mother greets me. "I've been waiting for you."

I shrug out of my backpack and say by way of explanation, "Lucy was talking to me after school."

She smiles at me; really *smiles* like she means it. "I'm packing up early. Julie has no problem with me closing early today."

Julie is Pastor John's wife, and she runs the church's business side. I barely know the woman as I don't really talk to anyone from the church even though I come here so much.

"Why? What are we doing?" I ask. We can't be going home this early, can we? It feels weird.

"I have a surprise for you, something I think you'll like," she says.

I look at her skeptically and don't say anything. She doesn't do surprises with me. Then again, maybe this is part of her atonement for everything she did to me. Or didn't do for me.

She packs up her purse and closes everything down on her desk. Then says, "Let's go," as she leads me out of the office. I toss my backpack onto the backseat of the car and climb in the passenger seat. I definitely know something is up when my mother turns away from home and heads towards the interstate.

"Where are going?" I ask.

"Brunswick," she says. "I'm taking you clothes shopping."

My eyebrows go up in surprise. So many questions fill my brain, and I can't pick which to ask. The first question I spit out is, "Can we afford that?"

She answers, "I have a little saved and we can spend some of it." She doesn't look at me, focused on the driving she is, so she doesn't see the shock on my face. "Not much," she adds, "but some."

"So . . . where are we going?" I ask again.

"The outlet mall."

I blink. That might not be my style, but there's bound to be *something* there I would like. "Can I choose my clothes?" I ask.

"So long as they're not too revealing." Whatever that means.

We drive twenty-five minutes or so to the mall in Brunswick. The parking lot is not too busy with it being a Monday. There aren't many cars around the movie theater parking lot either. We park near an entrance and walk up to the mall doors. My mother leads me through the mall. It's not the busiest place, all malls seem to be dying, but there's a few people walking back and forth.

We spend the next two hours shopping at the few stores here. She takes me to JCPenney, my mom's favorite, before going to American Eagle and Rainbow. I don't go for bright and shiny objects, but I was able to find some jeans and some black tops I like. I just wanted clothes that more closely represented me and for once my mother didn't really argue. She didn't want me to do anything low cut or sleeveless, but that was fine with me. I just picked out what I was allowed to, and we moved on to the next store.

With the afternoon waning, we go back to the car laden with bags of clothes and other accessories. I still prefer my boots from my Witch days, but I picked out some other shoes I liked. I climb in the car and my mother drives us out of the parking lot.

We don't say anything on the way home, driving down I-95 back to Darien. My mother just turns on the Christian station and plays music she likes. I don't mind because I mostly tune it out anyway.

My mom parks in the driveway some thirty minutes later. I climb out of the car, grabbing my backpack and half the bags of clothes. Inside the house I drop my bags, and my mom does the same. We'll wash everything before I wear it so she's just going to take the tags off and throw them in the laundry. I head upstairs with my backpack.

I open the door to my room, and Ikthiel is sitting on my bed.

"Happy Birthday," he says, holding a cupcake he got from who-knows-where.

I drop my bag and go to him, throwing my arms around him and narrowly missing the cupcake. He chuckles and wraps his arms around me, his claws notably short today. It's a relief to see him after spending the day thinking about how my life has changed.

I shut the door to my room and go back to the bed, splitting the cupcake with him. We eat it together in silence, the companionship feeling extraordinary to me. I feel so at ease with him.

"Did you have a good day?" he asks, eating the last piece of cake.

I shrug. "It was fine. It was school. Mom took me shopping though," I add.

He looks taken aback.

"I know," I say, "I'm surprised too."

"That's . . . unusual," he says. "What did you get?"

"More clothes. Stuff I actually picked out."

"Stranger and stranger."

I finished my half of the cupcake and meet his gaze. He's looking at me oddly, like there's something he wants to say. Tension grows between us for a moment. Then, as abruptly as it started, it seeps away. He gives me a crooked smile.

We talk for a while more about my school and Lucy's present, which he likes, and how things went with my mom at the mall. Then I'm laying back in bed, tired from the day. I find myself drifting off next to him, his arms around me. I fall asleep like that, his presence providing safety and comfort.

An hour later, when my mom calling me to dinner wakes me, I find him still there, still holding me. I knew then that something had shifted in our relationship. I just wish I could put into words what has changed.

7

May 15

Penny

Spring passed quickly for me, which is a relief. I'll never be fully comfortable on Earth again, especially after all the places I've been. But the last few months have taught me to find some relief in the little things. Like the relief I get today.

Jean shorts and a T-shirt. It is the best concession I've gotten from my mother yet. The T-shirt is plain baby pink, crew neck collar, and short sleeved. The shorts are a dark, first-day-of-school blue denim, falling halfway down my thighs, the shortest length my mother would agree to purchase for me. I study myself in my full-length bedroom mirror and consider the outfit. There are a few other pieces like it on the bed, some khaki shorts and more T-shirts, but nothing feels quite as good as this first outfit.

The color of the shirt and the shorts do not match my dark personality. I suspect if I had free reign over my clothes, I would probably dress somewhat goth. But there is nothing I can do about this. I just have to accept it until I turn eighteen and can do what I need to do. I can technically get a job now, but I have no transportation other than magic, and that might get to be noticeable. Out in space, I have so many credits built up that I probably would be set for life when I finally leave Earth again. For now, I just have to scrounge and save and let my mother direct my purchases.

I pull on some white canvas shoes that are starting to get dirty now but are still relatively new. I pull my hair back and consider my appearance once again. My hair is getting long. I like it long but it's getting overboard even by my standards.

Ikthiel appears behind me.

For a moment, I watch the demon in my mirror as he studies my appearance. He lifts a clawed hand to his chin and strokes it contemplatively. I wonder what he is thinking but choose not to pry into his thoughts. I hadn't really invaded his headspace since we got back from Widdershin all those months ago. I still seem to avoid it.

"You look different," is all he says.

"Good different?"

"Not quite like yourself," he says. "I miss you in your Witch's uniform. In your working gear that I used to see you in all the time." Of course, I miss that too.

He is referring to the utilitarian clothes provided by the Academy and worn by most Witches on commission somewhere. I loved those clothes. They were comfortable. Black pants that fit perfectly, a long-sleeved T-shirt in black, and a military-esque jacket in steel gray, all tied together with sturdy black boots and whatever other equipment was needed. The fabric of the clothes adjusted based on the climate you were in. So even in long-sleeves I never felt overheated, even in the jungles of Nahnu-beit.

"It'll work," I say. "It's getting too hot for those skirts to be honest. I missed wearing shorts."

Ikthiel comes over and runs his claws through my ponytail. His claws, today at least, are shorter than I usually see. They don't quite curl back to the fingertip like they did when I first met him. I wonder about that sometimes, but like most things and most curiosities I don't ask.

"What do you feel like doing today?" Ikthiel asks.

I turn around and face him. I have grown a few inches since I turned fifteen and he doesn't quite tower over me like he used to. His dark eyes study me, and I wonder again what I would hear if I pushed just a little and listened to his stream of thought.

"Aren't you supposed to be training me or something?" I ask sarcastically.

Ikthiel smirks. "I mean, we could do that, or we could do

something fun."

"Like what?"

"You don't travel much anymore. I figured I would take you someplace you haven't seen yet," he says.

My eyebrows go up. Not what I was expecting but then again I never quite know what to expect with him.

"What do you think?" he asks.

It's Saturday. My mother is downstairs working on the books for the church. I don't have homework because it's all done. I don't see why I shouldn't have some fun.

"Ok, where do you want to go?"

"I was thinking someplace nearby," he says. "And desertlike, given your attire."

"What, like Arizona?"

"I was thinking more Utah. Arches?"

I feel a smile come on my face. "Alright. Let's tell my mother and go."

I take his hand and lead him downstairs to where my mother sits at the kitchen table, her laptop out and a deep look of concentration on her face. She looks up when we walk in and takes a sharp breath at the sight of Ikthiel. Her eyes go to my hand in his, but I don't let go of it. Something rebellious in me dares her to think what she wants.

"We're going out for a couple hours," I say, glancing back to check with Ikthiel on the timeframe. He nods and I continue, "We're gonna be in Utah."

"Utah," she says. Her eyes sweep my attire. A resigned look crosses her face. "Be careful," is all she says.

Ikthiel wraps an arm around my waist, and we teleport out.

I blink once, twice. The view is incredible. We stand on a precipice along what is clearly a trail overlooking the iconic Delicate Arch. There are tourists around but none of them notices us. Anyone who saw us appear would just assume they hadn't seen us a moment earlier.

Ikthiel takes my hand and leads me away from the tourists to a place where we can take in the view and talk. I suspected he wanted to talk when he suggested such an Earth-centric location.

"How are things with your mother?"

"I can't say they're worse, but they're not much better either,"

I answer in a convoluted way. After a pause I add, "I don't know if they can get any better."

"Has she spoken with your father?"

I flinch at the mention of him. Few things can scare me these days. Few things are as terrifying as the Kolvat. My father is one of those things. "No," is all I say.

"Good," he says. "If she ever does, or if he reaches out, tell me."

I nod. I don't say anything else on the topic. I just mentally shove my feelings aside, my jaw clenching with tension. Ikthiel puts an arm around me, probably trying to comfort me.

"How about the rest of your life? How are your friends?"

I shrug. "I don't see them as much as I would like. I'm glad they're allowed to come over, but it's not the same. It's never going to be the same." I fall silent realizing that that statement is the truth. The truth I can't escape. Earth would never be the same for me. And my relationships here would never be the same either.

His claws squeeze my upper arm. "It's not forever," he says.

"Isn't it though? I haven't heard from Alicia Cole for months," I say despairingly. "I feel trapped here."

Even with all my power and all my abilities, I am still confined to Earth. The only times I have been off-world have been when Ikthiel has taken me somewhere. The moratorium on powers remains in place because of its attractiveness to the Kolvat. I feel shackled by the restrictions. And a simmering anger grows inside me with every day that passes. An anger I thought I had left behind in the ashes of Widdershin.

In August, it'll be a year since I've been back home. It'll be a year since I set foot on a spaceship. Since I was surrounded by Witches. Since I practiced my power openly. I feel so disconnected from that time. If not for my frequent visitors, it would soon fade to memory. I would soon let go of the past that changed me.

"Do you want me to try to talk to Alicia Cole on your behalf?" he asks.

I clench my jaw. I'm angry that anyone would have to advocate for me. But I also know it would probably fall on deaf ears coming from a demon. I'm not sure.

"You can try," is all I can think of to say.

I lean into Ikthiel's arm and stare at the devastatingly beautiful landscape. Having gone so many places all over the universe, it is still astounding to me how beautiful Earth really is. And I had no intention of returning home when I left over two years ago. To be able to enjoy this place is a privilege.

"We should go back," I finally say. I'm not in any hurry to return home. No, it's not that. I'm just feeling sad and alone right now, even with Ikthiel for company. I just want the familiarity of my room.

"You'll get out of here soon," Ikthiel whispers, pulling me into an awkward side hug. "I promise."

Given that he's the only one who has taken me off-world for the entire time I've been home, I believe his promise. We stand and round a bend to a deserted part of the area. He teleports us back to my street.

For a moment I just stand and stare at the two-story house my mother bought after the divorce. I just stand and stare at the symbolism that is this house. To me it symbolizes the ending of a tortuous era of my life. Of a time when the abuse infected every ounce of my life. It also symbolizes the trap I'm in. The way I'm stuck here.

I shake off my feelings and head into the house with Ikthiel in tow. I have no time for hate.

8

June 13

Penny

The letter arrived in my email connection like usual. But the contents are not the usual contents.

To: Penelope Williams
From: Alicia Cole
(via Google Offworld Exchange)
Copy: Talus Fairneau
(via Google Offworld Exchange)

Hi Ms. Williams,

I hope you are well, and your circumstances are safe. I am writing to connect you with a historian of sorts who will be visiting Earth in the next month. Talus Fairneau will be doing some work on Earth. It is my hope you will work with him on the project he is researching.

His specialty is the old Weapons of the past, the ones forged in the early days of the universe. Most Witches have even forgotten they exist or attribute them to myth. However, we have reason to believe that they are real and that one of them is in your home quadrant. It is our hope that you will be able to help locate one of these weapons. We believe they may be of use against the Kolvat.

I have taken the liberty of including some research he recommended. I have expanded your access to the Witch's net, allowing you to research at liberty to complete the work. I encourage you to use it.

While the moratorium on your power still exists, we believe you can safely use it in small doses. We have since discovered that regions where you did not use the full brunt of your power are of no interest to the Kolvat. Earth should be safe for the time being. I would not push it too far though. Know the limitations you have and please continue to respect them.

Please contact me with any questions relating to the power blockade. And feel free to connect with Talus for any help you need on his research.

May your Spark be a blessing,
Alicia Cole

I read the letter probably half a dozen times before I believed its contents. It had been a month since I had last seen Ikthiel and we had spent time at Arches. Time here at home flows so differently for me. And I can't believe that now I'm getting what I wish for: a purpose.

Out there in space, out in the universe, I felt like I knew what I was doing. I had purpose. I had dedication and motivation. Down here, on this old planet, I find myself wandering and unable to figure out where to go. I find myself alone.

I shake my head to jolt myself out of my thoughts. I would have to reply to the letter sooner rather than later. But there is no hurry. Talus Fairneau would not be here for a while it seems. I'm just not sure I like keeping people waiting. I'm known for being prompt after all.

Something in me snaps into place and I feel like my old self for a moment, the version of me that is a powerful and respected Witch doing work all over the universe. I don't feel like the trapped version of myself, handcuffed in power and kept sequestered away from everything I know and prefer.

I pull up my laptop and go to my Gmail account. From there, I activate the extension that allows the email to feed into the Witch's network, a little button with the letters "GOE" on it. I tap out my reply. I reread the email over for clarity.

**To: Alicia Cole
(via Google Offworld Exchange)
From: Penelope Williams
Copy: Talus Fairneau
(via Google Offworld Exchange)**
Hi Ms. Cole,

Thank you for reaching out and thinking of me. I am available at your earliest convenience and ready to work with Mr. Fairneau when he arrives in our quadrant.

Thank you for the reminder about my power restrictions. I am glad that I can use my power in small doses. I would like to increase my training if possible as I am still untrained and not adept in certain basics like other Witches are. Please let me know if you can increase my tutoring.
Thank you,
Penelope Williams

Short and sweet. I hit send and let the message go into the ether. Gmail says "sending" for a solid minute before it converts to "sent", but that's only to be expected when sending something to wherever Alicia Cole is at the moment.

And just like that, the feeling of my old self deflates out of me, like a tire losing its air pressure. I sink back into my desk chair and grumble inwardly at the restrictions and the possibilities of being stuck on Earth for the rest of my natural life. I feel like a discarded piece of fruit.

Anger swells in me in a way that feels uncontrolled. I had been just resigned to my fate for so long that the anger I carried with me had been kept at bay. But now that I've had a reminder of what it was like to be a free-roaming individual, I seethe at the restrictions on me. I haven't even seen anyone besides Ikthiel in months. I don't know what's happening with Altair or Firrl or the rest. I don't know *anything,* and it completely irks me. What am I supposed to do? Sit on my hands and do nothing?

I get up and start pacing my room. I feel like every nerve in my body jangles with the unspent power I carry. Frustration washes over me, and I can't help but punch my pillow. How stupid is it to keep their strongest Witch and greatest asset locked away on a lonely, backwater planet instead of using me to fight the war? What's it going to take to get me out of here?

The doorbell rings downstairs, but I ignore it. Mom's home and she can answer it.

I go to the window and look outside at the streetlamp that's currently off. It's not dark enough yet for it to come on, but I think about all the times when it's been on and Ikthiel has stood under it like a wraith. A shadow to haunt my space and keep me safe. I think about how he's the only one I've been able to rely upon in the Witch world. I really do wonder where the rest of them have been.

"Penelope! You have a visitor!" my mother calls from downstairs.

Surprised, I fluff my pillow compulsively and head downstairs. A familiar voice filters up to me on the staircase, and I pause for a moment listening.

"I haven't had much time to see her," the voice says. My heart leaps into my throat.

I jog down the rest of the stairs and turn a corner.

Altair.

Immediately and uncharacteristically, I go to him and hug him for all the life he's worth. His timing is impeccable. He seems taken aback by the hug but goes with it. He wraps his arm awkwardly around me and pats my back.

"It's good to see you, Penny," he says.

I pull back from the embrace and study him. He's grown again and now has to be six feet or taller. All that low gravity he lives in must be giving him the extra height. But he doesn't seem to be struggling with Earth's heavier gravity.

"What are you doing here?" I ask him.

"I just came to visit you," he says. "Is there somewhere we can talk?"

"Yeah," I say. "Come upstairs."

"Will you stay for dinner?" my mother asks, clearly being hospitable though I'm not sure why. Maybe it's because Altair is obviously human. Maybe it's something else. I don't know.

"I would like to," he says, following me to the stairs.

A moment later we are in my bedroom, and I'm closing the door so my mother can't overhear us. Altair looks around at my room. He's been in my room before, but not since I've moved back to Earth and I've made it more my own. My mother did most of the decorating, but actually took my direction on some things. So, there are posters of space on my walls and my bedspread is a blue galaxy pattern and the books on my shelves are somewhat more to my taste. He studies the titles for a moment before pulling out my desk chair and sitting down. I sit cross-legged on my bed, my sock feet fidgeting. I can't seem to sit still these days anymore.

"So, tell me everything," I say to Altair. My obvious interest in him takes him aback. I am not the person I was when we sat together on Kaldreesa, and I refused to ask him questions. I am not who I once was.

"I am living on a planet called Klaxion," he begins. And I listen to him tell me all about his new life there. He doesn't have a foster family anymore. Not since Imfra-Rega died. Not since Kaldreesa was destroyed. But he doesn't mind that. He is older than me by a year or so, depending on how you count it, and he is living on his own now. But he still keeps in touch with the Rega family survivors and knows they are doing well. I'm glad for that.

It's more of his story than I ever would have gotten or asked for, before the fall of the Academy. I have been isolated so long that my ability to live without stories, without people, is suffering to say the least. I didn't realize how important it was to me to meet all those new species and all those new people everywhere I traveled. Just hearing about them from Altair is making me nostalgic for my time on Widdershin.

"How are you doing?" he asks as he finishes his story.

I shrug. "About as well as can be expected," I reply honestly.

"I feel claustrophobic here. Like I'm trapped and alone."

"I can understand that," he says with sympathy in his eyes. "I'm not allowed to use my power as freely as I was before . . .," he pauses, "well, before. But at least I'm out there. I know you feel like you're not doing anything."

"It's frustrating," I agree.

"Do they have you doing *anything* besides training?" he asks.

I tilt my head to the left as I consider my words. It's not classified so I might as well tell him. "They have me looking for one of the Weapons," I answer. "At least I will be when I meet with the researcher who's coming here to Earth to look."

Altair's eyebrows go up. "You mean the Creation Weapons?"

I pause. I consider what he just said. And a flare of anger swells up inside me threatening to spill over. "You mean to tell me, you're not even from this universe, and you *know* about the Weapons?" I ask with hostility in my voice. The hostility is not directed at him. It's directed at everyone in charge who dares keep me in the dark.

He raises his eyebrows and shakes his head. "They really have to give you all the information," he says. "I can't believe they're keeping their best chance at defeating the Kolvat ignorant of everything. Is Ikthiel still getting history texts out to you?" he asks.

"You know about that?"

"He asked for my help," he explains. "Who do you think has been stealing some of the oldest, hard-to-get-to texts?"

It occurs to me that I need to ask the demon more questions than I have been.

"So why are you really here then?" I ask.

A smile lights up Altair's face, drowning out the concern he showed only a moment ago. "I'm going to take you on a little adventure," he says. "I know you have seen all of your solar system by this time. So, I'm going to take you a little further away."

"Oh?"

"Let's go visit an old friend of yours." He grins as he asks, "Would you like to see how Fahum is doing?"

My eyes widen. Fahum. My handler from Nahnu-beit. My friend. The person who saw right through me and liked me anyway.

"You really mean it?" I ask, breathless at the idea.

"I do," he says earnestly.

"Let's go!" I say leaping off the bed and reaching for my shoes.

Altair laughs. "You'll need to change. It's winter there now," he says."

"In the *jungle*?" I ask incredulously.

"Oh yeah," he says. "Nahnu-beit is quite unique."

"Alright then you're going to have to wait a minute," I say.

Altair laughs and sits down on my bed. I rifle through my dresser drawers for my warmest winter clothes and pull them out. I step into the bathroom and change my clothes down to my socks, pulling on jeans and a long-sleeve shirt, thick socks, and a hoodie, the only concession to normal clothes my mom made back in January. I come back out, and I reach into my closet and pull out my puffer coat that comes down to my mid-thighs. We had planned to go to Vermont to visit my mom's old friends for Christmas, but the plans never panned out. She doesn't really have family and with her job not having great pay, she just couldn't afford to make the trip. But she had bought me the jacket already, a fact which I am grateful for now.

I open my door, the jacket slung over my left arm. Altair raises his eyebrows at me and asks, "Ready?"

"Always," I answer. I'm ready to get off this damp rock of a planet and see my friends again.

We head downstairs, and I explain to Mom where we're going. She narrows her eyes but has the decency not to argue. I guess she must have warmed up to Altair somewhat. Probably because he's human. It feels a little . . . speciesist to me?

We head out the front door like somewhat normal people and walk to the end of the street. There we stand behind some trees, hidden from view on most sides, and Altair takes my hand. I feel safe alone with him, as safe as I feel with Ikthiel. For a moment I feel like there are eyes on me, but the feeling passes.

Altair smiles at me kindly as we disappear from Earth.

9

June 13

Lucy

I don't know if I can believe my eyes. I don't know if I can believe what just happened.

I rounded the corner and saw them. Penny and some tall guy I don't know who looks to be about our age. Maybe he's a friend of hers from school? Maybe. They were holding hands, and I was about to call out to them when they just . . . *disappeared.*

Dumbfounded, I just stand there staring. I don't know what I just saw. Can something like that be explained? Was it real?

I hustle over to the spot where I saw them and look around. After about five minutes of inspecting the area, I feel sure that there is nothing out of the ordinary with the trees or the ground there. My parents are scientists. I should be able to logically reason my way around this one.

Did they just go into the woods?

No, I would have seen them go that way.

Was it a trick of the light?

It's broad daylight. I can't blame it on that.

No. They *disappeared.* They just vanished.

I close my eyes and shake my head. I don't know what to make of it. I don't know what they did. But I do know one thing.

Penny is keeping a secret.

Aimlessly, I head in the direction of my house. I am so lost in thought that I don't even notice Bryce until he is right on top of me. Until I almost run smack into him.

"Lucy?" he asks softly, concern wrinkling his brow. "What's wrong?"

I'm honestly, completely at a loss for words. I really don't know what to say.

"Are you ok?" Bryce asks, his hands on my shoulders now.

I stutter but can't seem to find the words.

"Tell me what happened?" Bryce says.

I can't quite make eye contact with him, and that seems to be freaking him out more. So, I look up at Bryce, replaying everything in my head and thinking through the words. There are no words to describe it really. I don't know what I saw. I can't explain what I saw.

"They . . . *disappeared*," I whisper.

"Who? What do you mean? What happened?" Bryce asks frantically.

"Penny . . . and . . . someone," I struggle to get out. "They just *vanished*."

Confusion takes over the concern on Bryce's face. He's going to think I've lost my mind. *I* think I've lost my mind. What does any of this mean?

It means secrets.

The thought keeps invading my head. The idea that Penelope could be keeping a big—no, *huge*—secret from me is stunning. But what is she hiding? What does it mean that she and that boy disappeared into thin air?

"Lucy, you're scaring me," Bryce says, pulling me into a firm embrace. "What happened? What did you see?"

My eyes shut involuntarily, and I squeeze them to block out the image and the thoughts. What exactly did I see? What could it possibly have been?

I feel like my brain is breaking.

I swallow, my mouth suddenly parched in the afternoon heat. But I don't think it's the heat that's made me thirsty.

I force the words out.

"I saw Penny with some guy," I start. Bryce's eyes follow mine, confusion still warping his features. "They were standing there one second and gone the next."

"What . . . like they went around the corner or something?" Bryce asks, not quite getting what I'm saying.

I shake my head. "No," I answer, "like they *weren't even there*." I make eye contact with him. "Like they were there one second and gone the next." His eyes study mine. I don't know if he's going to accept what I said. But he has to. I need someone to believe me when I say what I just saw. And I trust Bryce with everything I've got. I just hope he trusts me the same way I trust him.

"Do you believe me?" I ask. I barely believe myself.

"Are you sure that's what you saw?" he asks, some skepticism in his eyes. I wouldn't trust it the first time either. How could I? It's impossible to explain and even more difficult to comprehend. How could someone just vanish?

Faithfully, I nod my head. Words fail me.

"Where did this happen?"

"Just by her house," I answer. "Near the trees."

"And you're sure they didn't just go into the trees, and you missed it?" he asks.

Doubt colors my mind. For a moment I replay it over and over in my head hoping to see something different. But then I shake my head. I firmly say, "No. They *disappeared*."

Bryce nods his head, studying me carefully. Whatever he is looking for, he must have found it. He says, "Let's get you home. If Penny is gone, we can't ask her about it now."

I swallow again. "You believe me?"

Bryce gives a wan smile. "I don't know what you saw," he admits, "but I trust you and your judgment. If that's what you say you saw, then I believe you."

A tight breath escapes me. I didn't even realize I wasn't breathing while I waited for his reply. It's like he's my sanity check somehow. It's like he is the logic and reason I feel has escaped me in the past hour. Has it only been an hour?

Bryce turns me and puts an arm around my shoulders, directing me to my house. I walk robotically with him, not really thinking about anything else. I'm in shock, I think. My body feels like it's in shock.

We get back to my house and head inside. My parents are still at work, thankfully. I don't know what I would say to them about the state I'm in. Bryce plants me on a kitchen stool and pours a glass of water for me. I take it gratefully, gulping it down like my life depends on it. He takes the empty glass back and refills it. I drink it down, slower this time, my thoughts calming down now that I'm inside, out of the heat, in a safe place. My shoulders, filled with tension since I saw what I saw, are finally relaxing slightly.

"Better?" Bryce asks.

I nod and set the glass on the counter.

"Now, let's go through it again," he says softly. "What *exactly* did you see?"

So, I describe it to him. From the moment I stepped around the corner and clamped eyes on Penny. To when I was about to shout. To the way she was holding that boy's hand. Everything. Right up until I saw them disappear. And I describe it as best I can. Like they were there one second and simply *not* the next.

Bryce follows my description, listening attentively, waiting for me to finish, taking it all in. He is quiet when I finally stop talking. He pours a glass of water for himself. I watch him drink the water and lean against the kitchen counter. I take in the details of him, his faded blue t-shirt and the jeans that seem too heavy for such a warm day. I even look down at his faded white Converse. The utter normalcy of his appearance stands in stark contrast to the description I've just laid out. I don't know what he's thinking.

"Say something," I ask. "Tell me I'm crazy or tell me I saw what I saw. *Something.*"

His brow furrows like he's trying to solve a calculus equation. Finally, he lets out a sigh. "I believe you," he says. "I don't know what you saw, but I believe you saw what you saw." He shakes his head. "I almost don't believe it, but I believe you."

"I thought I was going crazy," I say.

Immediately he shakes his head. "No, I highly doubt that," he says. Then he pauses like he's considering his next words very carefully. "Do you think we should ask her?"

"Penny?" I say. "I don't know. Won't she try to deny it?"

A feeling I can't identify twists his features. "Don't hate me for saying it," he says, "but I think we need to catch her to ask her."

My eyes widen and the bottom drops out of my stomach. "You mean, like, *spy on her*?" I ask.

Bryce nods. "Think about it," he says. "If she's been keeping this huge secret from you, from *everyone*, she's not going to give it up easily. She's not just going to come right out and tell you what's going on with her."

I tilt my head to the left. He has a point. "I guess you're right. It just feels wrong to even talk about."

"I know," he says grimacing. "But I don't have any other ideas."

I sigh heavily. "It would certainly explain a lot about the last few years," I admit.

"What do you mean?" he asks.

"You didn't really know her before she went away," I say, "but she changed in the last few years. Like *something* changed." I pause, trying to think through how I'm going to say this. "Her parents got *fanatical* about religion where Penny was concerned. They got crazy about it. I went to that Jesus camp they sent her to, and it was crazy. But even before that, they didn't like me hanging out with her anymore." I shake my head. Talking through this is only making it make more sense. "And there're the injuries."

"Right, like when she broke her arm," Bryce says ruefully.

"Right." I let out a tight breath. "I think she's been hiding this secret for *years*," I finally say. I grab the glass of water and take another few gulps. No amount of water is going to change what I just figured out. My best friend has been lying to me.

I shake my head and look Bryce in the eye. "I mean, where did she even go that whole time last year?" I ask without expecting an answer. "I don't think it was at a school for the gifted after her parents put her through so much. I don't think she was at a Jesus school either, given her demeanor coming home."

"What do you mean?"

"She seemed almost . . . defiant . . . at being back," I explain. "Like she would rather be back at wherever she had come from."

"You think it was a better place?"

"Away from her family? I have no doubt."

"Then why is she back with her mom?" Bryce asks.

"A good question."

Bryce walks over and puts his arms around me. "We'll find out. And then we'll ask her."

I nod against his chest. It's a good plan, even if it feels wrong to spy on my best friend.

But if she's been lying to me all this time, can I still really call her my best friend?

The worst part is I think I know the answer to that question. And I don't like the way it's going.

.

INTERLUDE

The matter sits before them, imbued with the oldest magics
known. The rock of a planetoid contains several barren landscapes
which prove to be perfect for the work to be done. So, they stand,
the pair of them, in an open rocky plane with the turning galaxy
above illuminating the night sky. The planetoid's hot, bright sun
flickers unstably in the distance, a small star that is young even by
the universe's standards.

"Where did you find the metal?" the child asks.

The matter is heavy and hums with power, the kind of power
older than all their kind. It is a dull gray with some hints of green
and purple in the mix, the metal not being pure but a blend of
several metals from a star's death.

"Sourced from the starfire forge," the parent says.

They carefully wield the matter into the forge of energy. The
consecutive rings are quiet for the moment, the power still in them
as the parent inserts the metal. The block is misshapen, a blob of
possibilities poised to be formed into something new. That is
exactly their purpose here: to build something new. The child
doesn't understand why yet, but they will. Someday, in a time when
they are all forgotten, this creation will still exist. Only something
older than the magic in the metal could destroy it.

The parent takes their time bending the forge's energy to their
will, that being their primary talent. The child watches as the matter
shapes and shapes again into a long rod with a heavy block at the

top. With some further manipulation, the block turns into a perfect hexagonal prism. The rod extends down from one of the six sides with the two hexagonal ends pointing away from the rod.

The forge slowly quiets down as the parent hushes the energy there. They keep the power in check and reach into the forge with a long appendage to remove the hot metal. They are made of transcendent matter-energy, so the heat from the metal never bothers them. They take the forged creation and carefully set it in a matter-energy holder to cool to a stable state. The cool of space will invariably stabilize it in less than a turning of the planet.

"What happens now?" the child asks.

"Now we wait for it to be stable enough to carry with us," the parent says.

"What are you going to do with it?"

"Give it to the Talented that are worthy," they answer. "For only the worthy will be able to wield it. Its power will only come to fruition at the greatest hours of need."

"Just like our powers."

"Just like our powers," the parent agrees.

They watch the flickering sun blink as it passes over the horizon. They watch the turning of the galaxy, the bright swathe of stars illuminating the dark of night. Then they watch the flickering sun return and the time has come.

The parent takes the matter creation from the holder and shuts down the forge finally. The last remnants of energy that make up the forge blow away in the stellar winds coming off the sun and the neighboring stars. They gather their remaining things and shut everything down.

The time has come to leave and deploy the Weapon where it is most needed.

PART 2

10

June 20

Penny

My visit with Altair was well timed. I needed the reminder of the good people out there with whom I still have connections. Altair is one of those good people.

The thing that really irks me about my whole situation is the neglect. I feel like I'm being neglected by the whole of the Witch community. It feels unfair given how much work I've done for them, never mind being critical to the saving of the Academy's Witches. I have hardly any communication with the outside world. Altair's visit sort of hammered that home to me.

The following day I got a message from Talus Fairneau, this one not copying Alicia Cole.

To: Penelope Williams
From: Talus Fairneau
(via Google Offworld Exchange)

Hi Miss Williams,

I am happy to be working with you on this project. I will be in the area next week to discuss the project and what your role will be. Can you meet with me on your planet at the coordinates listed below? I am interested in discussing your training and I hope to show you some examples of the older Tools.

May your Spark be a blessing,
Talus Fairneau

His message listed some coordinates that correspond to an empty field in Kansas. Unsure what I would find when I met him, I decided to concentrate on what I could control. So, I spent the rest of the week doing research on the Weapons from the material he sent as well as diving into the Witch's library resources for some history. There wasn't much to go on, but I had enough to help me understand the mythology of the Weapons.

No one knows who exactly forged the Weapons, but it seems like several were forged at different places in the early universe and allowed to scatter as the expansion continued. I cannot begin to fathom the creatures from the early expansion days. No more than I can begin to fathom the creator of the first spell matrix. I think about that spell matrix often, and I want to go back. But I would need Ikthiel to take me, and he's been busy this month. That spell matrix, however, predates the forging of the Weapons. That's as far as I can compare the two without going back. So, I take the time I have and study.

When the day arrives that I have to meet with Talus Fairneau, I decide to use the spell Altair left with me for teleporting. It's not directly going against the moratorium on my power. I'm using a spell matrix, instead of my raw power to move. I haven't really used my raw power to move since that day on Widdershin. I've not really teleported much either. Just piggybacked on Ikthiel or Altair.

I pack my backpack with a few things like notebooks and my laptop. I figured out how to give my laptop infinite charge by pulling energy from its surroundings, so I never feel the need to worry about it dying. All the research I got from Talus Fairneau is on there as well as some research I pulled from the Witches' library. With my communicator on my wrist, I leave my cellphone on the charger and head downstairs.

My mother is home early from work today, the office being closed early on Thursdays. There is no evening service either, so it doesn't make sense for my mother to stay late. It's only noon and she just got home. She's sitting in her usual place at the kitchen counter when I come down, reading something or other on her laptop and taking the occasional notes. She looks up when I come in.

"I'm heading out to meet with a researcher," I explain when she gives me a querying look. I don't really have to explain to her what I'm doing, but I find that some details keep her from prying too much.

"Where to?" she asks, setting her pen down and picking up her coffee.

"Somewhere in the middle of nowhere Kansas."

"Kansas," she says incredulously.

I shrug. "I didn't pick it."

"Who are you meeting with? The demon?" she asks.

"No, this professor of history named Talus Fairneau. He's kind of an archeologist for Witch artifacts, I guess you could say," I answer with a bit of a smile on my face. Talus Fairneau feels like the kind of person who is Indiana Jones in the flesh.

"Oh!" she says in surprise. She clearly wasn't expecting that answer. "Well, be careful. Will you be home for dinner?" she asks. She no longer requires me to be home for dinner, but rather *asks* that I do. Our talk back in January really helped even my footing with her.

"I'll try to be," I answer. "I'm not sure what all we're doing. I was just assigned to him to assist his research."

She raises an eyebrow. "I didn't know you were interested in history," she remarks.

I smile. "I'm not, generally," I answer. "But the history of Witches is interesting, and the artifacts we're looking for are equally so."

She nods, accepting everything I said even though it clearly makes her uncomfortable. "I'll see you tonight?"

"Yes," I say. "I'll message you if I'm going to sleep elsewhere." I say that as a courtesy. Again, it's easier to keep her in the loop than spread vitriol between us.

She thanks me and wishes me luck before turning back to her laptop. I head out the front door and go to the little stand of trees where Altair and I blinked out just a week ago. I pull up the little spell matrix on my communicator and project it out. I put in the coordinates Talus Fairneau sent over. Finally, I activate it, and I'm instantly transported to the middle of a cornfield in Kansas.

The heat smacks me in the face. It's only ten in the morning but it's already as hot as in Darien. I look around me in the corn and listen to the sound of the wind. A rustling to my right draws my attention. I move that way, weaving through stalks of corn and trying not to damage anything. The corn is big but not quite full grown and ready to harvest yet. Not that I know anything about farming. I just figure it's not ready because of the smaller size of the ears.

I come through the corn to a road I can only assume is cut through the corn for some piece of farming equipment or other. Dust kicks up on the dirt road as the breeze picks up to proper wind. I block my eyes for a few minutes, protecting myself from the dust. Then it dies down just as quickly as it started, and I look around in the direction of the rustling noises.

I head into the next patch of corn. I continue to walk carefully until I come to a small opening, a place where a large piece of farm equipment, an irrigation machine perhaps, sits taking up space. There, next to the irrigator, is a man with light brown hair and a medium build.

He stands up at the sound of me and turns to face me. I'm met with the face of a middle-aged man with moderate lines and wrinkles in his face. The edges of his hair are turning gray, but he is still young. He is dressed in jeans—no idea how in this heat— and a blue, short-sleeved button-down shirt. The shirt pocket boasts a piece of equipment that can't be from this world. I don't know what it does, but no Earth object is made from that metal.

His entire appearance is fake.

I stare at him for a moment and let my Witch sight cut through the facade. He is not human at all, but some humanoid species, which explains how he is moving with such ease. The skin below the facade is blue speckled with brown, short hair on his head a darker shade of blue-black. Eyes, green as the cornstalks around us, peer at me with interest and I smile up at him, hoping to break the tension.

"Penelope Williams?" he asks.

"Yes," I answer. "You're Talus Fairneau?"

"Yes." He leans over and adjusts the piece of equipment I only just noticed. He turns a few knobs on it and adjusts a dial. A tiny screen shows up, bright enough to be read even in this full daylight. He taps a couple spots and waits, then turns back to me when he seems satisfied.

"You weren't followed or spotted?" he asks.

"Of course not," I answer, slightly indignant that he would suggest I would be that clumsy.

He smiles at me, a surprising genial look. "I meant no offense," he says. "With planets like this, you never know." He extends a hand and I shake it, feeling the leathery inhuman skin below the illusion. It's a good illusion, but I've seen better. Harilsen's is better, for example.

"Are you ready to get started?" he asks.

"What are we doing?"

"First, we're going to finish taking readings here on Earth," he explains, taking on a teacherlike demeanor. I wonder if he's ever been a professor of any kind, as he strikes me as one. "I suspected at one time that there was a Weapon here on this planet."

"Here?" I interrupt him, incredulous at the suggestion.

"Yes," he answers. He looks over at me and gives me a wry smile. "I'm sure you're curious as to why there is no mention of it in all that research I sent you."

"Yes."

"Well, it's in my own personal research that hasn't been published," he further explains. "I didn't see the need to publish supposition."

He really is like a scientist. At least his approach is scientific in nature.

"When we've ruled out Earth, we'll start on the surrounding galaxy," he says. "The Weapon in question is either in this galaxy or the two orbiting little ones."

My jaw drops. "How do you know that?"

"I've spent my life's work seeking these Weapons," he explains. "Xirlans live one of your millennia," he adds.

I blink. "How old are you?" I blurt out without thinking about politeness.

He smiles at me again. "You are as blunt as your reputation promised."

I look at him ruefully.

"By your accounting, I am considered middle-aged," he says. "I won't tell you more than that."

My gaze goes to the equipment behind him, as it starts beeping.

"Ah, good," he says. He waves me over and shows me the readout. "It's detected a fragment of the original ore," he explains. "Just one instance, thankfully. Earth is a large planet to have to comb through section by section."

"I thought Earth is small?" I ask.

"Small for a rocky planet, but I come from a smaller place."

I think back to Nahnu-beit and the smallness of that planet and wonder if my scale for size is a tad biased.

"Well, let me pack up the interferometer and we can get going," Talus Fairneau says. "I bet you didn't expect to do field work on your first day."

I shake my head. "No, I didn't," I answer. "Where are we going?"

"About three shizkas north from here." At my blank stare, he says. "Oh, you don't know what a shizka is. Let's just say it's close."

He pushes a button on the interferometer, and the whole machine folds down automatically into block no bigger than a cellphone. He reaches down and picks it up, pocketing the device.

"Take my hand," he instructs. "I'll do the jump."

Since I don't know where we're going, I can't argue. I take his hand, and we're jerked uncomfortably into a new location. Shaken by the transit's roughness, I bend over and heave a few deep breaths. *What was that?*

"Oh," he says regretfully. "I guess you aren't used to a Xirlan tesseract."

"Is that what that was?" I ask, a bitter tone to my voice.

"Sorry," he mutters. I've hurt his feelings.

I look up at him and see the pain on his face. "It's ok," I say. "I'm alright."

He smiles at me.

I straighten up, the waves of nausea passing. That was awful.

"Now what?" I ask.

"It's around here somewhere," he says looking around. We're in another field, but this is a natural one. Just grass and boulders spread out around us. I'm not sure we're in Kansas anymore.

"So why this metal?" I ask. "Is it the early creation metal you talked about in your papers?"

A light comes into his eyes. "It's more than that," he says, pulling the interferometer out again. He hits a button and it casually pops back to its full size. "You know how you can imbue magic into matter?"

I nod. The communicator on my wrist is prime example of the applications.

"Well, I postulate that it wasn't always that way," he explains. "There had to be a *first time* the magic was successfully bonded to matter." He taps the controls on the interferometer. I watch his expert hands flick over the controls. "There had to be a first."

"Like there was a first spell matrix," I say, thinking immediately of the first matrix in that strange space.

"Precisely!" He looks over at me with pride. "Why do you think that matter is different?" he challenges me.

I think for a moment. Everything from my reading suggests that the Weapons were created early in the universe. Could matter have been different then? "Is it because of when they were created? Is there something unique about the early matter?"

Talus Fairneau gives me a sly smile. "What would make it different?"

"Besides the presence of antimatter?"

"Besides that."

"Well, it wouldn't have degraded much yet, would it?" I ask. "Entropy wouldn't have had enough time to cause decay."

"Correct," he says. I breathe out. "The matter is purer than anything else in the universe. The magic imbued in it froze it in its original state."

I blink. "What do you mean froze it?"

"I don't know exactly how, but the power within the early matter must have staved off or significantly slowed entropy," he says. "The power must be protecting it from decaying somehow."

"And that's what we're looking for?"

"Not looking for," he says. "Found."

He walks away about ten paces and kneels down. I jog to catch up to him. I watch in fascination as he plunges his hand into the ground as if it were made of air. Then he rifles around for a few minutes before pulling his arm back out. And in his hand in nothing more than a shard of metallic rock.

"Hm," he says, studying the specimen. He hands it to me and asks, "What is your assessment?"

I take the piece of rock and use all my senses—including my Witch ones—to look it over. The rock is definitely different. You wouldn't really know by looking at it, but it hums with a different energy. It is definitely old, older than anything I've ever held. But it's not what we're looking for.

"There's magic in it, sure," I say, "but it's not a Weapon."

"How can you tell?" he tests me again.

"There's no intent in it. Nothing in it suggests there was intent in its forging," I answer. "Plus there's the fact that it's kind of just a lump of rock." I hand it back to him.

He chuckles at my assessment. "You are correct." He pockets the matter, and we head back to the interferometer. He breaks it down and says, "We have a few more places to check out, some of them clear across the planet."

"I'm game," I say with a shrug.

He holds out his hand, and I brace myself for the next jump.

The rest of the afternoon unfolds like that. He jumps us to the next location, and we scour the area for little fragments of metallic rock. We inspect them, analyze them, and store them for further research later. He eventually pulls out a pouch from his back pocket, and we start bagging the rocks from as far away as India. We're standing on the top of a mountain in Africa, freezing I might add, when he finally calls a stop.

"I can't detect anything else," he explains, raising his voice over the harsh wind. "Whatever's left isn't big enough to be detected."

I nod, my teeth chattering in the cold. "Can I go back home then?"

"Yes," he says. "I'll reach out to you in a few days when I have the analysis done."

"Ok!" I shout.

"Do you need me to jump you home?"

"No!" I say immediately. My stomach can't handle another jump. Instead, I tap on my cold communicator and pull up my home coordinates.

"Thanks for including me!" I shout.

"Thanks for coming!" he replies.

I hit a button, and I'm back behind the trees outside my house. I look around for a few moments and then head into the house. Mom left a note on the kitchen counter saying she went out for groceries. It's barely four o'clock. I pour myself a glass of water and contemplate making hot chocolate to warm up. But I'm already feeling warm enough. The heat of Georgia is doing its job.

Ikthiel appears in the kitchen, and I smile at him.

"How was your first day?" he asks.

Before I can answer, we're interrupted.

There's a knock on the door.

I set my glass down in the sink and go to answer it. I open the door to find Lucy and Bryce standing there. I smile at them, but then I take in their expressions. They're both angry. My stomach sinks.

"What is it?" I ask.

11

June 20

Lucy

The following week Bryce and I made a plan. A plan that didn't sit well with me but felt necessary. We had talked through everything over and over again, and I came to the same conclusion every time: Penny is lying. I hated myself for thinking it. Worse, I hated myself for believing it. But there was no way around it. She is definitely hiding something. And I decided I want to know what.

"What do you think it is?" Bryce asks, as we sit crouched in the woods beside Penny's house. We can see her whole house from here, at least this side of it, and we can see the spot she disappeared from the other day. She isn't home, but I suspect that will change shortly.

"I don't know," I say. The possibilities are endless. Is she a mutant? Is there a secret realm I don't know about? Is magic real? I can't say what it is. And did she just disappear, or did she teleport or something similar? That's the real question. There was no trace of her when I looked last week. But there was no trace of her in that spot.

Bryce adjusts the tiny tripod he has his phone locked into. The phone's camera is set to wide angle and encompasses the whole of the house. He's actively recording and every now and then stops the video and restarts it so we'll have an easier time finding the shot later. Provided we catch her on video. Which I really hope we do. It's probably the only way she will tell the truth.

"It looked like she disappeared," I say, "but it could be teleportation or something."

"You think it's a power?" he asks. Bryce likes fantasy stories more than I do. He used to read them more than I did. So I've been relying on him for the vernacular. I'm too much of a scientist's daughter to think that way.

"Why not?" I say. "I'm just curious if it's hers or the boy's."

"Good point."

"And if it is the boy's, then who is he, and how do they know each other?"

Bryce nods, his gaze going from the camera to the house. It doesn't seem like anyone is home in the Williams's house. It's that time of the afternoon before adults get home from work. That weird part of the afternoon when time feels like it drags, and you struggle to find ways to pass the time. A slight feeling of guilt courses through me. I should be doing anything instead of spying on Penny's house. I promise myself when all this is over, I'll apologize to Penny and always do my homework on time.

An hour passes in companionable silence. I can tell Bryce is getting stiff from sitting still for so long, but he doesn't complain. He apparently wants to be here as much as I do. He wants to see what I saw and get answers. I asked him about that when he suggested our little stakeout, and he just said that he hated to see anything upsetting me. He wanted to help me figure this out, so I didn't have to worry anymore.

I doubt I would stop worrying. What has Penny gotten herself into? What kind of life is she leading that she can disappear in an instant? She's still my best friend, even if she is lying to me. I have every right to know the truth, especially since we always say we're not going to lie to one another. She's clearly been lying.

I find my eyes boring into the tree she disappeared behind. I am sitting there behind the bushes just staring at the tree's bark when it happens.

Penny appears out of nowhere.

My hand goes to Bryce's arm immediately. I hear his sudden intake of breath, nearly silent but loud enough. We watch as Penny looks around her, seems satisfied there's no one, and heads to her house. Together we hold our breaths as she goes inside, completely oblivious to us in the bushes.

"Did we get it?" I whisper to Bryce. I'm not sure why I'm whispering.

He stops the recording and rolls the video back to the last few minutes. We watch entranced by the little screen as there is nothing but the tree one moment and Penny standing there a fraction of a second later. There is no doubt.

"I believe you," he whispers. "And we have proof now."

I nod at him.

"What do you want to do?" he asks me.

My stomach sinks immediately. *What do I want to do?* My mind runs through my options all over again. And there's really only one option to take. Confront her.

"Should we confront her now?" I ask Bryce.

He tilts his head to one side and seems to be thinking. His eyes go vague, and I wonder what he's considering. "Do you think now is the right time to do it?" he asks.

I look back at the house and let out a tight breath. It's about four in the afternoon right now. Her mother won't be home for another hour and a half. We have a window of time where we know she's alone. Or at least we think she's alone. I look at her living room window and see a shadow go across for a moment. She's definitely home.

I get up and say, "Let's go."

Bryce stands up, gathering the tiny tripod and his phone. "Are you *sure?*" he asks.

I look at him, my mouth set in a line. I feel my jaw clench. "She's lying to me," I say, "and I want to know why. I want to know what she's hiding."

Bryce squeezes my hand. "You may lose her friendship over

this," he says softly.

I swallow the lump in my throat. "If I let her keep lying to me, I know I will."

"You can't stand the lies, can you?" he whispers, walking with me towards her house now.

"I really can't."

We fall into silence as we come to her front door. For a moment I just stare at it, at the wood door and the secrets that must wait beyond. How much does her mother know? Is this why her last few years have been a living hell?

I raise my hand and knock. Bryce straightens up next to me, holding the phone in his hand ready to go. I really hope we don't have to show her that clip. I feel so slimy for spying on her.

The door opens.

Penny smiles in recognition as she sees us standing there. Her eyes go back and forth between us, seeing our expressions, and her smile fades. Confusion and concern flit in her expression. "What is it?" she asks, misgiving in her voice.

I straighten up. "I want to know what you're not telling me," I begin. "I want to know what's really going on."

"I don't know what you mean—" Penny lies.

I interrupt her, "Yes, you do." I hold up my hand to stop her from protesting again. Fear fills her eyes. "I want to know why you were sent away for a year. I want to know why your parents disowned you, but suddenly your mom takes you in again. I want to know what you did that warranted your parents' hatred of you." I take a deep breath. "And I want to know how it is that you can disappear into thin air."

Her jaw drops. Her eyes go back and forth between Bryce and me. She shakes her head as if in disbelief at first but then with purpose as if to deny everything. She's about to lie to me again. She's about to kill our friendship, now that I've confronted her.

"C'mon, Penny," I say angrily. "I went with you to that Jesus camp and suffered every punishment with you. You *owe* me an explanation."

Her face turns rueful. "I don't owe anyone anything," she

huffs. "And I don't know what you're talking about. My parents just turned on me," she says. "And I sure as hell can't '*disappear*'," she growls.

"You're lying," I say, hurt welling up inside of me. "I can't believe you're lying to me." I shake my head feeling tears starting to gather in my eyes. Then I let the ax fall. "Show her," I say to Bryce.

"Show me *what?*" she says angrily.

"This," Bryce says. He holds up his phone. I can't see it from my angle, but I know the video of her appearing out of nowhere plays on the screen.

The color drains from her face. "It's a trick of the camera," she lies again.

"Stop lying to me," I say. "This isn't the first time I saw you disappear or reappear out of thin air. This is just the first time I caught it on camera."

Her eyes widen and she flushes, her arms crossing over her chest with her hands clenched into fists. She looks ready to fight. For half a second, I think she might punch me.

"Stop lying to me," I say. "We're supposed to be best friends."

Her features soften slightly. Oddly, she tilts her head slightly to the left and almost looks over her shoulder. There's no one else home though.

"I know we're best friends," she says softly. "But there are some things that I can't tell you."

"Like everything apparently? Like the *truth?*" I ask, the words coming out in a hiss.

Her eyes close, resignation on her face. I honestly don't know what she's going to do. I don't recognize my best friend at this moment. I don't recognize a single thing about her. Her posture, her stance, the clothes she's wearing. None of it.

Penny opens her eyes, her gaze sharp as it falls on me. "You, I trust," she says. She turns to Bryce, "But can I trust you?"

Bryce and I exchange a look. "I can vouch for him if that means anything," I say. "I trust him."

She scoffs. "I know *you* trust him. Can I?" she says. "Can you keep a secret from everyone in your life? Can you hide something even from your parents?"

Bryce looks at me, and I just watch him. This is up to him now. This is his show as much as it is mine. If he doesn't answer her and say the right thing here, we could be back to square zero.

"I can keep it from them, from everyone," he says. "I would never hurt Lucy by betraying you."

Penny looks startled at the words. They must have been the right words, though. Her features soften, and she drops her protective arms.

"Penny," a male voice says from deeper in the house. "Bring them inside."

She nods and purses her lips. "Try not to freak out," she says as she steps aside to let us in.

Bryce and I exchange another look as we step across the threshold. Penny shuts the door behind us but doesn't turn the lock. I walk around the corner of the foyer to the wide doorway opening into the living room. A figure stands there. He is a man, at least that's what I would describe him as, but he has pallid skin and dark, dark hair. His clothing is utilitarian and all black. His boots leave an indentation in the taupe carpets. My eyes go to his eyes, for a moment wondering why she would say not to freak out. Then I see his hands.

At the end of each finger, a thick, black two-inch-long claw curves away like an elongated crescent. My mind goes immediately to science as I list every creature in my memory with claws like that. He is not a creature of biology. He is a creature of mythology, something I am sorely lacking in.

Bryce takes my hand. His eyes are on the killer claws. His jaw clenches with something akin to fear but laced with anger. Is this the secret Penny has been hiding?

Penny goes to stand next to this man, if we can call him that, and watches our reactions. She is not smiling, but she is no longer angry. She just looks weary, resigned to the events of the afternoon somehow.

"They're taking it better than I expected," she says to the man.

"Indeed," he says. "But they don't know the full truth, yet."

His words startle me. "What full truth?" I growl.

Bryce's hand squeezes mine. I find comfort in knowing I'm not alone confronting Penny.

"The truth of why my parents hate me," she says. "Everything you asked starts and ends with Ikthiel." She gestures to the person beside her.

"What do you mean?"

"I have a story to tell you," she says. "One I think you'll believe."

She gestures to the couch, and Bryce and I move that way. When we are seated, she begins.

"One day, when I was ten years old, I walked home through the woods behind Dollar General . . ."

12

June 20

Penny

"And that's why I went away last year," I conclude. "I went to learn."

I look over at Ikthiel, who is leaning on the doorway, subtly keeping Lucy and Bryce in the house while appearing casual. He is a better mind-reader than I am, and he is studying Lucy and Bryce with great interest. When he meets my eyes, he gives a slight nod, the only indication I'm getting right now that things are going without too much of a hitch. The moment Lucy called me out on my lying, I knew I was going to tell her the truth. Secrecy be damned. What has hiding from my best friend ever gotten me?

I am sitting on the couch with my back to the front windows. The sheer curtains are drawn, dappling the light somewhat. It's after four o'clock, but we still have an hour before my mom gets home. I don't need her walking in on this and interrupting . . . whatever this is. I need to somehow salvage this conversation, this friendship. Something.

They're taking it rather well, Ikthiel says silently. *I can't really read the boy well, but she's an open book. And she's accepting what you've said.*

Thank you, is all I say in reply. Knowing Lucy is handling it well is making me feel slightly better, even if having Ikthiel read her mind feels like cheating.

"When did they pull you out of your parents' house? When you first moved in with your great-aunt?" she asks.

I nod. "I was living in a hotel for about a week and a half."

"Oh," she says. She knits her eyebrows together.

"Why did they pull you out of your parents' house then? Why not sooner?" she asks.

I take a tight breath. I had left out the part about my father beating me nearly to death. I hadn't wanted to dump too much on them all at once. But she's asking, so she should be told.

Ikthiel crosses the living room and sits next to me, taking my hand in his claws. *Tell her*, he says silently. I nod at him.

"My father beat me," I say. "Ikthiel saved me."

Lucy's eyes go wide. Her jaw drops and incredulity fills her face. "He *beat* you?"

"Yes," Ikthiel answers for me. The words seem to have died in my throat. "He nearly killed her. By the time I got there, she was in a pool of blood on the kitchen floor." I flinch at his description. So does Lucy. Bryce puts an arm around her shoulders.

She shakes her head. "How were you not in the hospital after that?" she asks.

"We have healers, good ones at that," I say. I always feel grateful to the Witch who healed me. I had only seen them once since, but I had done the uncharacteristic thing and thanked them sincerely.

"And it's a good thing," Ikthiel grumbles. "He nearly broke her spine." Anger flashes in his eyes.

"So, you're a . . . Witch?" Lucy asks Ikthiel tentatively.

I exchange a look with him, silently telling him to tell her the truth.

"No," he says. "I'm what is often called a demon. A Witch who . . . chose a different path." The explanation is sufficient if not complete.

He squeezes my hand letting me know he heard that.

"A demon?"

"Yes," he says. "We are considered dark creatures because of our choices."

Lucy shakes her head. "This is too much," she says. "You're telling me that you've been a Witch for, what, *five years* and you *didn't* tell me?" Anger colors her voice. Tears well up in her eyes, as well. Bryce says nothing but holds onto Lucy to comfort her.

"Yes," I say. "I know it's unforgivable, but I'm choosing to tell the truth now."

"Only because we found out," Lucy says ruefully.

"I *couldn't* tell you! You think I didn't want to?!" I nearly shout. "You're my best friend! I told them you could handle the truth, but they didn't believe me."

Anger crosses her face. "You should have told me anyway." She shakes her head, tears falling on her face. I can see the betrayal there. The sense that I've been hiding this from her for too long. "Why didn't you tell me about your father?"

I run a hand over my face. "I couldn't without telling you everything else." I shake my head. "I didn't want to burden you with it."

Lucy curses at me. "That's just crap," she says. "It's just a lame excuse."

"I would have told you, if I had been allowed to!"

"We'll never know now," Lucy says softly. "We'll never know what you would have done if I had never found out."

I clench my jaw, the uncomfortable pressure in my teeth feeling like a punishment I deserve. "I wanted to," I repeat.

"She did," Ikthiel says.

Lucy turns her angry gaze on him. "I don't know you, whatever you are," she says angrily. "So I can't accept that you won't lie to defend her."

I bow my head into my hands and then straighten up. "What do you want me to say? I'm sorry? I doubt that will cover it!" I yell. "There are rules that govern worlds like Earth. There are reasons why we're not known. There aren't even that many of us on Earth. And you know what would have happened if I had told you?" I ask with vitriol in my voice. "You know what they would have done? They would have simply erased your memory. Maybe even erased the memory of *me* from your life!"

"Don't you dare," she says. "You could have told me in confidence. It's not like I hang out with Witches! Except, *apparently*, I do!"

I stand up. Lucy matches me. Bryce matches her. Ikthiel rises to my right. This is *not* going how I hoped it would.

"Lucy, I can't lie to you anymore. I have a lot going on in my life, a lot to my story, you don't know," I say softly. "I can't be at odds with you over this. Do you believe me?"

"I don't know what I believe," she says, her eyes looking away.

"Do you believe I consider you my friend? My best friend?"

"What about him?" she says, gesturing to Ikthiel. "What is he to you? And what about that boy? And Firrl?" she says, her eyes widening.

"All of them are friends," I answer. "And before you ask, Altair—the boy you saw—is human. Firrl, however, is a fish species under the illusion."

Lucy's jaw drops. I had forgotten until that moment her obsession with fish. "And you think I wouldn't have wanted to know that? To *see* that?"

I huff extensively, blowing out air as if it will somehow blow away my troubles. "Yes, I did think you would love to know her, actually. And I told Firrl as much," I answer.

"Oh? And what did she say to that?"

"She told me to tell you," I admit quietly.

Lucy throws up her hands and turns around facing away from me. When she turns back, she looks flustered and angry as she says, "Well at least I know you don't listen to *any* of your friends."

My hands come up to my head involuntarily, and my fingers run through my hair completely destroying my ponytail. "Like I said, I was told to keep it quiet, even from you. I wish I could take it back and start over again. I would have told you the day I laid eyes on Ikthiel and Altair."

Lucy stares at me like she doesn't believe me. Because she doesn't. I've betrayed her, and I don't think there's any walking this back.

"Whatever you say," Lucy says quietly. The deadly combination of distrust and anger fills her voice.

"I mean it! I promise!"

Immediately, I know it is the exact wrong thing to say. Her eyes flash at me, and she says, "Don't use words you don't understand."

I bite my lips inward, sucking in a breath. I know I screwed up. I don't know how to fix this.

You may have to give her space, Ikthiel says.

Yeah, I got that.

"Whatever happened, whatever I saw, you weren't going to tell me," she says. "And I don't know if I can forgive you for that."

I look away, nodding and accepting that it's really her choice to make. "What can I do to make it up to you? I don't want to lose you as a friend," I plead with her.

Her lips go tight as she says, "I'm not sure what we are. But you've proven we really aren't friends."

"Please, Lucy," I implore. "I don't want to lose you over this." The tears in my eyes are falling now. The tears I can't hold back dampen my cheeks.

All she does is stare at me with hurt in her eyes. "You already have," she whispers and heads for the front door. Bryce follows her and I hear the door open and shut.

Once the door clicks closed, I lose it. I completely fall apart and find myself sobbing into Ikthiel's shoulder. I can't hold it together over this. I just lost my one true friend, the only person who supported me even in my darkest hours. She never knew what I was really going through, and she supported me anyway. How can I be losing her after all this time?

"She'll come around," Ikthiel assures me. "I read her mind. She wasn't sure of what she said."

I shake my head. "No," I sob. "She was angry and hurt. She left."

"She'll forgive you," he says.

I can't believe I'm getting comfort from a demon.

"I'm still capable of empathy," he rebukes me.

I'm not sure how long I cry on his shoulder, but eventually I pull back and sit back down on the couch. There's nothing that can be done. Lucy will either come around on her own or she won't. And I only have myself to blame.

The door opens and closes. For a moment I get my hopes up, but my mother comes around the corner. She is carrying groceries and freezes in the doorway to the living room when she sees us sitting on the couch. She looks at me, at Ikthiel, and back at me. "What happened?" she asks.

I swallow. "Lucy knows."

My mother tilts her head and goes to the kitchen to set down the groceries. Then she comes back to the living room and asks, "You told her?"

I close my eyes and shake my head. "No. She and Bryce saw me teleport," I explain. "They caught me."

"Ah," my mother says. "And she's angry because you didn't tell her sooner?"

I look at her and nod. How did she pick up on that so quickly?

"Did you tell her everything? Did she believe you?" she asks.

Again, I nod my head. "I told her most of it. She believes that I'm a Witch,   and I have powers. She's angry about the lying."

My mother is silent for a few minutes. "Well, you and Lucy have been inseparable since Kindergarten," she says. "She'll come around. It might take a while, but she will."

Is my mother actually trying to comfort me? This whole day has been bizarre.

My mother is careful to keep her distance. We aren't close after all. But she waits while I think about what she said.

"I hope you're right," I say. "Lucy was right. I should have told her sooner," I admit. "We used to tell each other everything."

My mother nods, sympathetically, I think. She seems to understand what's going on. With Ikthiel here, she's still tense. But she is having this conversation with me as a total shocker.

"You'll have to find a way to apologize at the level of the transgression," she says. "Pastor John always says forgiveness is a matter of one's ability to forgive oneself. She's probably as angry at herself as she is at you."

"What do you mean?" I ask. "How is she angry at herself?"

"Well, you said it yourself," she explains. "You're best friends. She's probably angry she didn't notice all the changes and ask you earlier. She's probably angry at herself for not being there—"

She doesn't finish the thought, but we both know what she's talking about.

I don't answer her. I look at Ikthiel and think about all the ways I've let Lucy down.

"Don't beat yourself up over it," my mother says. "It's not constructive. Find a way to ask her for forgiveness." She turns from the living room to head back into the kitchen but pauses. To Ikthiel she asks, "Are you staying for dinner?"

He raises his eyebrows. "Yes, if you'll have me," he says.

My mother nods and heads back into the kitchen to put the groceries away. I get up from the couch and head upstairs with Ikthiel on my heels. When we're alone, I softly shut the door and turn to him.

"Do you think she's right?"

"She's insightful," he says. "I'm not sure she's wrong. I'm also not sure what can be done about it. I don't have much experience with forgiveness. Except from you."

I blink. I think back to when he lied to me and when he healed me on Nahnu-beit. I think about the betrayal I felt that he had hidden that from me all those years. How did I get over that to still call Ikthiel a friend? I wish I had someone else to ask what to do.

"You will figure it out."

I plop down on my bed. He takes my desk chair in a move reminiscent of Altair's visit last week. I sigh. There's only so much I can concentrate on at once. Do I focus on getting Lucy to forgive me? Or do I focus on the conundrum of finding the Weapons? Both are important.

Ikthiel squeezes my hand. "We'll figure it out."

I nod in agreement, though I don't really see how. I may have just lost my best friend today and I honestly don't know how to get her back.

13

June 20

Lucy

I am furious. I march down the street in the general direction of home, with Bryce jogging to keep up with me. My hands are clenched into fists and my feet hit the pavement with angry strides. I don't know what to think. I just know I feel furious.

"Lucy," Bryce huffs out. He's not winded exactly but is struggling to keep up with the brutal pace I'm setting. "Let's get to your house. Let's get home. We can talk this over."

I shake my head. "There's nothing to talk over. She's been lying to me for *five years*," I hiss.

"And you've been friends at least twice that long," he argues.

We walk up to my front door and let ourselves in. Quietly, so as not to disturb my mother working in her office, we go upstairs and head to my room. I shut the door, and he sits down on the bed like usual. I can't sit still though. I pace back and forth, wringing my hands together or rubbing them on my face.

Bryce just watches me and gives me space. This is why I like him and care about him. He knows when to stop and let me just feel my feelings.

"I just don't understand how she could do that," I say, keeping my voice relatively quiet. I don't want my mother to overhear. As angry as I am, some sense of loyalty remains. I don't want to expose Penny, mostly because it's not my secret to tell.

"It sounds like she had to," he says.

I hate that he's defending her, but I'm not going to argue with my voice of reason. Bryce is and has been my voice of reason. He's cool-headed when I'm not. And I need him to be cool-headed right now.

"I still say she could have talked to me about it."

"And I'm not saying you're wrong," he says. "I'm just suggesting that we really don't know what's going on with her, even more so than a few hours ago."

"What do you mean?"

"I mean, yes we know she's a . . . Witch," he stumbles over the word, "but what does that really mean?"

I blink. "You mean like what does she do with the power she has?"

"Exactly," he says. "What is she doing with that demon? Or, what was his name, Altair?"

A rueful look comes over my face. "There's more questions than answers," I grumble. "She's given us some answers, but not the whole story."

"Not in the least," he agrees. "I think we've just hit the tip of the iceberg."

I sit down on the bed next to him. "You think I should talk to her," I say. It's not a question.

He puts an arm around my shoulders. "I think you should give it a few days, give it all the time you need," he says, "and then go talk to her."

"Why?"

"Because your friendship deserves that much courtesy," he says. And he's right. He's so right I hate it. But I know he's right.

"Bryce!" I hear my mom call from downstairs.

Hauling myself off the bed, I open the door and shout, "He's up here! What is it?"

"Is he staying for dinner?"

Bryce looks at me and shrugs. "I could eat." He could always eat.

"He's staying!" I shout back.

Then I shut the door and go back to the bed.

My fish tank bubbles in the silence between us as I contemplate his words. On the one hand I think he's right. He's too right, really.

But on the other hand, I'm frustrated and angry and hurt. Penny lied to me. She knowingly lied even when she was confronted. And then she had the gall to say she had no choice. We left her the option to tell us the truth. I trusted her, and that trust has been badly broken.

"What are you thinking?" Bryce asks. As if he doesn't already know. He can read me like an open book.

I shrug. "I'll talk to her, but I definitely need some time."

"Take all the time you need," he says. "I definitely think you should text her tonight, to let her know you're not completely mad."

I grimace. "I *am* completely mad," I say. "I'm just calming down now."

"Well, tell her you'll talk to her in a couple days, that you need time to cool off," he suggests. That's an idea I can get behind.

I pull my phone from my pocket and type out the message.

Still mad. Need space. Will talk to you in a few days. I have questions.

Bryce reads it before I hit send. I stare at the phone for a few minutes. Then I look up at Bryce. He is smiling at me, his hand rubbing between my shoulder blades to make me feel better.

"What is it?" I ask him.

"I'm proud of you," he says. "You didn't back down and even now you're taking the higher ground."

I make a face. "The higher ground is not always fun."

"I understand that," he says, "but give yourself some credit. You had many shocks today, her betrayal only one of them. You stood your ground amidst all that. I'm proud of you."

I lean into his shoulder and smile. I can't help it. He completely disarms me. "Thanks," I say. I let out an emphatic sigh. "I guess we should talk about something else."

"Absolutely not," Bryce says startling me. "I mean . . . she has *powers*," he whispers. "She's a Witch! How can we talk about anything else?"

I laugh softly at his enthusiasm. He didn't say a word the whole time I confronted Penny, a fact I appreciated at the time. But I couldn't tell how he felt about the whole thing. Until now.

"You're excited about this, aren't you?" I ask him. I'm annoyed at that, but I can't fault him. He's such a sci-fi/fantasy nerd.

"I am," he admits. As if I needed the confirmation. "You have to understand I've thought about this my whole life practically," he says. "Dreamed about having powers and flying like a superhero. The fact that *exists* and someone I know *has* it? That's incredible." He shakes his head and I laugh softly. "I really mean it. I want to know more."

I can't help but smile at his enthusiasm. I can't help but feel better, feel the anger deflate out of me as he talks like that. He's just acting like himself in the face of all this. Of all the people I know, he probably would take this revelation the best. And I have to admit, he's not the only one excited by the idea. I'm more excited by the aliens than by the powers. The fact that Firrl, someone I *met*, is an alien baffles me. I wish I had known and could have talked to her about it! And the fact that she's a fish species according to Penny? I look over at my fish tank. I would love that.

"Are you feeling better?" he asks.

I bark a laugh. "I'm still a bit mad, but I've calmed down now," I answer. "I need a couple more days to cool off before I talk to her probably. Just so we don't get into a screaming match again."

My phone goes off then. It's a text from Penny.

Understood. I can wait.

I show it to Bryce. The phone pings again. A second message comes through.

I really am sorry. I didn't mean to hurt you.

I let out a breath. I know her, and I know she means it. I know she's reeling from this as much as I am. I can't imagine having a secret exposed like this. Having my life flashed out for people to see. I don't know if I would have taken it as calmly as she did. And I don't know that I wouldn't have lashed out for the spying. Because that's the thing that gets me. She didn't say one word about us spying on her. Like she didn't even feel hurt by it, or didn't want to bring it up. She didn't mention it at all. And I wonder if she felt like it was justified after everything she did. I wonder if it was some form of self-punishment or an attempt to be exposed by using the not-exactly-protective trees to teleport. I wonder.

But there's no time to wonder about that now. There's nothing I can do but work through my feelings, probably with Bryce's help, and figure out how to forgive her.

"You ok?" Bryce asks, watching me closely.

I shrug. "I think I will be," I answer. "I don't know if I'll be over it for a while though."

"That's ok," he says. "You're allowed to be upset and angry and all the rest. You just can't wallow in it."

"Wise words," I jibe him.

He laughs. "I'm a very wise person," he says with feigned seriousness.

I grin, unable to keep a straight face.

"Lucy! Come help with dinner!" my mother calls from downstairs. It's already almost six o'clock. Amazing it's only been a couple hours since everything changed.

I get up and open the bedroom door. "Coming!" I call back.

Bryce gets up and gives me a hug. He holds me for just a second, and I feel calmer at his touch.

"Let's go," I grumble.

And just like that we have to drop the conversation and leave it for later. We head downstairs knowing we're going to have to save any speculation about her powers for later.

The anticipation is killing me.

14

June 20

Penny

I sit with Ikthiel in my bedroom just feeling whatever I'm feeling after that whole explosion with Lucy. Is she wrong? No. Am I wrong? Probably not. But I feel so wrong in this. I feel completely at fault and completely and totally *wrong*.

"Stop beating yourself up," Ikthiel says.

I shake my head. "She's not wrong," I say. "That's the worst part." I get up and start pacing like I have been for the past twenty minutes. I'm so annoyed with myself for not telling Lucy about this sooner. Like from day one.

"Stop it! You can't keep wallowing in self-pity about this," he says somewhat harshly to me. If I didn't know him, I'd say he was being mean. But I do know him. And I know he's trying to shake me out of my self-doubt and self-loathing. I know he's trying to fix me in the way he knows how.

"I'm trying," I grumble. I keep pacing my bedroom in frustration and anxiety about how everything is going. My bedroom is tiny, and the most I can do is take three steps in either direction. So I keep circling and it's not helping.

"Why didn't I just do it?"

"I don't know," Ikthiel says. "It's not like you're a rule follower. You have broken the rules before."

I stop in my tracks and look at him. "No, you're right. I have broken the rules before. Look at when I brought you to Widdershin."

"I brought myself, thank you," he says tartly. "But I take your point."

I shake my head ignoring his words. "No, that's not it." And I sit down on my desk chair abruptly as I realize what it is. "I didn't trust her to believe me."

Ikthiel stares at me impassively. He can read my mind, so I have no doubt he's following my thoughts, but I feel the need to speak them out loud anyway.

"I didn't think she would believe I have powers," I say. "I didn't trust her to keep it a secret either."

"That's pretty bad," he admits.

I look him in his dark eyes. "I know," I say. "I feel like a terrible person."

"You kinda are," he says.

"Thanks. You're so helpful."

"I try."

"Well, I don't know if I need helpful right now," I mumble. "I need the truth." I let out an exasperated breath. "Could I have gotten away with telling her? All those years ago, could I have done it?"

Ikthiel seriously considers the question rather than answering it right away. He seems to be mulling it over, leaving me sitting in silence and annoyance. Finally, he says, "It depends on when we're talking about. Right away? They would have found out and had her memory wiped. So, it wouldn't have made a difference."

"What about later?" I ask. "What about after I moved the boulders, after I could use my power?"

Ikthiel gives a wry smile, no doubt thinking about that first time I managed to use my power. "Then you might have been able to hide it. You might have been able to shield her well enough to hide her knowledge."

It's an admission I know is the truth because I can feel it in my gut. I can feel the way I betrayed her over and over again. The way I let both of us down.

"So I could have told her."

"Yes."

The words hit me like a tank. Hit me in my core and take me

down. I don't know what to say other than, "I'm sorry."

"I'm not the one who needs the apology," he says. "But you already apologized to her. You just have to let her come around on her own."

"And let her break off our friendship if she wants to," I say ruefully. I may have permanently damaged our relationship over this. And I *know* she's right that I owed her an explanation.

I think back to kneeling with my head on the banister at Jesus camp. I think back to her telling me in the courtyard why she decided to go with me. We're friends. The best of friends. The kind that doesn't abandon each other or lie to each other. We're those people. Why would I ever think it would be ok for her to not know?

"Well, she knows now," Ikthiel says, answering my thoughts. "What she does with it remains to be seen."

I shake my head. "I know she won't tell anyone."

"Do you?" he asks. "Are you *sure?*"

I must admit I'm not, but I don't want to say it out loud. I don't have to though. He looks at me with a cocked eyebrow and I know he heard my thoughts. "Bryce is the wildcard," I say. "What he'll do, I'm not sure."

"I don't know either," Ikthiel says. "Like I said, he was difficult to read. I didn't get much off him, but what it was leaned positive. I think he was just intrigued at the idea of you having powers."

I give a crooked smile. "He is a bit of a sci-fi nerd," I explain. "He probably already believed powers exist and aliens are here on Earth."

Ikthiel snorts. "It's not like he's wrong."

I giggle. A genuine giggle. "No, he's not," I chuckle.

"The best you can do is wait them out."

My wrist communicator buzzes. I look down and see a text from Lucy. My breath leaves me. She actually texted me.

> **Still mad. Need space. Will talk to you in
> a few days. I have questions.**

I read the message to Ikthiel.

"Well, that's promising," he says. "And I wonder what questions she has."

I snort. "Knowing her, she'll want to know about Firrl or about how our powers work." I shake my head. "Stuff I really can't explain to her well."

"I can help," he says, giving me a wry smile.

"I'm sure you freaked her out enough. I'm sure she's discussing the existence of you with Bryce right now."

"Don't you have a text message to answer?" he gripes.

I sit staring at her message for a while, not really thinking, just feeling. What could I possibly say to her? An apology almost seems ludicrous. This is too big for an apology. I need make it up to her somehow, but I have no idea how. I have no clue what could possibly appease her.

And I don't really want to appease her. I want her forgiveness, not her tolerance. I want her to be my friend again. Because right now it certainly doesn't feel like we're friends. It feels like our friendship is broken.

I sigh. And I type out my response.

Understood. I can wait.

I pause and think about it for a few seconds. Then I type out a second message.

I really am sorry. I didn't mean to hurt you.

I don't expect a reply.

I take off my communicator and set it on my bedside table where it usually sits to charge. Ikthiel watches this and then holds out his arms. I move to the bed, and he hugs me.

"I know that was hard," he whispers.

Vulnerability does not come easily with him. He's expressly told me not to be that way with him. But in the past year or so, we've learned to have that in our relationship. We've learned to show that side to each other. I'll never forget him walking up to me on Widdershin when I was comforting Altair. I'll never forget his tolerance and understanding. Maybe that's why, above all other people I know, I trust Ikthiel with the knowledge that Penny knows. I know he won't turn her in and get her memory erased.

"I would never," he says. "I don't subscribe to their notions of security." He grins at me. "Nor am I a rule follower."

"Uh huh," I say. "We all know that."

He pulls me closer and holds me in my grief. That's what this is. Mourning for a relationship I thought would never change or end. But clearly it has changed if it hasn't outright ended. Her text gives me some hope, but I don't trust hope. I haven't trusted hope in a long time.

"What did Talus have to say?" he asks.

I straighten up. I almost forgot about my outing with the professor. "We chased down some fragments of early matter from the birth of the universe. Some fragments imbued with power," I explain.

Ikthiel raises his eyebrows. "I forgot that such things could exist."

"Most people don't believe the Weapons are real or that they exist anymore," I answer. "Talus feels differently."

"So I gathered."

"Well, he says there's a Weapon in our galaxy or nearby," I say, explaining badly.

"I do wonder why it would be out here," he says. "But there's no telling what the forgers of the Weapons thought."

"There's no telling who actually hid them either."

"I wonder about that," he says. "The myths around them are vague as to why they were hidden. I actually wonder how many of them are still out there."

"How many were there?" I ask.

"I don't think anyone knows."

"Hm," I mutter. I wonder what Talus Fairneau thinks about that.

I hear my mother calling from downstairs. I get up and open the door and stick my head out and yell, "What!"

"Dinner!" she yells back.

"Are you staying?" I ask in a quieter voice.

"Sure," he says. Ikthiel gets up from my bed and follows me downstairs.

After today, I need a bit of normalcy. As normal as a demon eating with my mother can be anyway.

15

June 21

Penny

There is nothing consoling about my dreams that night. I find myself awake again and again in the pre-dawn hours, sweating through my sheets and angry at myself. I will eventually heal from this, but I hurt myself as badly as I hurt Lucy with my lying through omission. It will take time for me to feel better about this. If I ever do, honestly.

I've been bitter before, and I feel bitter now. I feel like my choices have brought this on me. And I lay in my bed staring at the ceiling at 6AM and wondering about the changes I could have made in the past several years. I think about everything I went through from the day I saw Ikthiel for what he was, and I think about how different my life would have been with Lucy fully in the loop. With Lucy able to help me cover and hide and protect myself.

I glance at the clock again. It's still barely after six. I groan audibly and roll over.

"You really should try to sleep," Ikthiel says.

Startled, I look over at my closet door where he's leaning casually. I flop my head back on my pillow and roll my eyes. "I *did* sleep."

"Not well."

That I can't argue with. I tossed and turned so much my sheets are in a tangle. I'm lying in my pajamas with the sheet barely over my legs. I just feel restless.

"Do you want my company, or should I leave?" Ikthiel asks, the courtesy getting me to look at him strangely. He's been acting so differently since Widdershin that sometimes I wonder if he's the same person as the one who asked for my power to give to his fellow demons. I wonder how much he's changed too.

"No, I don't mind the company," I answer, sitting up and using my pillow to prop myself against my headboard. The headboard is a new thing. I wouldn't have had one when living with both my parents years ago. They took everything away from me back then.

Ikthiel comes and perches at the foot to my bed, kicking off boots and crossing his legs underneath him. For a moment he looks almost fully human. His claws aren't even that prominent this morning, shorter than usual and blunted at the end.

"You're still hurting," he remarks. It's not a question.

"Yeah," I say, "but I'm not sure there's anything I can do about it. Just let Lucy have the space she needs."

Ikthiel's face looks guarded, as if he's holding something back. "I don't want to upset you further."

"What do you mean?" I say, alarm shooting through me.

His expression turns rueful. "Well I have some news that I doubt the higher up Witches will tell you," he says. "I doubt they've remembered the kind of weapon you are and how useful you could be."

I sit up straighter and cross my legs under me mirroring his posture. The tone of his voice suggests it's something serious, so serious he hesitates to dump it on me. "Is that why you came yesterday?" I ask.

He nods. "But with everything that happened with Lucy, I decided to hold back till today."

"You can tell me."

He sighs as if he is about to dump something huge on me and feels badly about it. I almost read his mind then, almost pry into his thoughts the way he's always in mine. But he's a demon, and I'm not. I might get along well with demons, but I'm not going to let myself become one.

"There's a problem," he says.

I roll my eyes and say, "Of course there is."

He huffs at me and says, "It's serious. It's at the Edge."

My eyebrows knit together. What could *possibly* be worse than the Kolvat at the Edge?

"The Kolvat are there, of course," he says in answer to my thoughts, "but there's something else. Something is eating away at reality itself."

Confusion floods my mind. "What do you mean 'eating away at reality'?" I ask, slightly indignant that something else could be happening out there.

"Well, it's like this," he begins. "You know how spacetime can be a tangible thing, not matter exactly but something between matter and energy?" I nod. I know this, yes. Witches can manipulate spacetime with our powers. Some Witches, like Altair, can manipulate it to great effect. "Well, it seems like something is . . . *feeding* on it," he says tentatively. It's like he can't even find the words for it.

"And it's not the Kolvat?" I ask.

"No," he answers. "They feed on true physical things. This is feeding on spacetime itself," he says.

A shiver runs through me, and suddenly I'm freezing in this June heat. "*Feeding,*" I repeat. "On the fabric of reality." It feels far-fetched but I know better than to contradict Ikthiel. He's typically honest with me.

"Yes," he says. "Shredding it almost."

"But how is that even possible? It makes no sense. How is the universe vulnerable to something like that?"

"I don't know," he says, and his expression tells me he is telling the truth. "I only know what I saw and sensed and what the Witches know."

"Show me," I say, extending my hand to him.

He obliges. He takes my hand in his and shares his thoughts with me. He shares the image of the Edge and what's going on there.

My sharp intake of breath tells him that I'm seeing it.

The Edge moves around, it changes all the time. It's not like there's a physical edge to the universe from our perspectives. I'm not sure how it works from another universe's perspective, but this is how it is for us. So I'm seeing a place I don't recognize, a solar system with twelve planets that I can count from where I am.

Hanging in space above the sixth planet is the familiar roiling, turgid blackness that I've come to associate with the Edge. But this is warped even for this part of space. This distortion turns my stomach.

As I watch, the distortion shimmers a violent purple, light leaching out of the open space over the planet. The warping of space reacts to the incursion with a bright flash followed by stillness. The Edge is quiet where the incursion touches it.

I shudder at the sight. The Edge should not be frozen. It's an expression of the tension between two universes. It's a bizarre and uncomfortable sight, but the space should move. It should pucker and roil in response to the bending of reality. It should not freeze. And this is frozen. Frozen where something clearly took a bite out of it.

I let go of Ikthiel's hand. "What does it mean? What's causing it?" I ask.

"I honestly don't know," Ikthiel answers. "And neither do the Witches. They are just as confused as you feel right now."

"Then what are we going to do? *Is* there anything to do?" I demand of him. He can't just bring me a problem without having some idea what it consists of.

"I don't know," he admits. "I really don't know what we're going to do about something that can do this. I don't even know what it is."

A sinking feeling overwhelms me. His words concern me. I have up till now viewed Ikthiel as my best source of information. He has been the one to help me understand history and how Witches work and everything else. He knew about the first spell matrix. He knew about the Edge. How does he not know about this?

"This is beyond my knowledge," he says in answer to my thoughts. "I only see the future within the bounds of the universe. I can't see anything from beyond."

This is news to me. Not that I really know everything about Ikthiel in the first place. I feel again the unfairness of how well he knows me and how little I know of him.

"What do you want to know?" he asks softly.

"As much as I can handle," I answer. It's not really an answer.

He sighs. "I want to tell you everything," he says, "but I'm not sure what you can handle."

"Eventually, I hope I can handle everything. Eventually, I hope we can be completely open with each other." But I know that "eventually" is not now. So I let it go.

"Do you want to sleep?"

"Not really," I answer. "I'm too awake, and I'm still beating myself up."

"Then you really do just want company," he says.

I nod at him. "This is going to sound stupid, but can we cuddle?"

A wry smile comes over his face. "I can't remember the last time I was asked to cuddle," he laughs softly.

It's still barely seven in the morning, and I haven't heard my mom get up yet. She doesn't have to go in on Tuesdays till almost lunchtime so I know she won't be up soon. I stretch my legs out and pull the covers back, readjusting the pillow so I can get comfortable again. Ikthiel takes his jacket off revealing a long-sleeved shirt of the high-tech material I miss from the Academy. It's soft to the touch as he lays down next to me and wraps an arm around me, his shorter claws causing no discomfort this time.

"Why do you want to cuddle?" he asks softly.

I clench my jaw. He can read me like a book, so he already knows what I don't want to say out loud. But I still say instead, "Because of everything that happened yesterday with Lucy and feeling rotten overall."

He pulls me closer, wrapping his second arm over me as I settle in. "I know how you feel," he says, though I'm not sure what he's talking about. I just let it go.

The sun is up in full but my curtains black out my room with only a sliver of light coming in around the edges. I lay my head on Ikthiel's shoulder and think back through my whole relationship with him and the trust we've gradually but steadily built. I think about all my relationships, even the ones that are over and long ended because of death. Like Rebecca Whitney and Imfra-Rega, both of whom opened themselves to me and took me in in ways I had never experienced. I think about all those people who tolerate me despite my curmudgeonly nature because I am useful and I choose to be helpful. And I think about Altair and Firrl. I think about how they both see me as a friend despite my best efforts otherwise. For the first time in a long time, I see myself for who I really am. A coward.

I'm a coward who doesn't want close relationships because I'm afraid of getting hurt again. Am I justified in feeling how I feel? Of course, I am. After my father nearly shattered my spine with his boot, I'm perfectly justified in being angry and mistrustful. What I'm not justified in doing is never growing from that pain and never learning to trust again. I surprise myself by realizing I do in fact trust people. But I clearly didn't trust Lucy.

I trust Ikthiel to be an open book with him. I trust him to read my mind and know me, really *know* me. I trust him to be my friend, my confidant, my protector, and my teacher. I trust him to be so many things in my life that I doubt I would be the same without him. I doubt my ability to function without him.

So finally, after the sun is up and the light coming in my room is bright, I whisper, "Tell me everything."

"Are you sure?" he whispers back.

He knows I'm sure, but I love him for asking. "I'm sure."

"Alright," he says.

And he begins to tell the story of who he was and who he is.

16

June 26

Penny

The following week I'm waiting in the backyard for Talus Fairneau to come get me. He said it's faster for him to just tesseract us where he needs to go, so I'm bracing myself for the jarring journey. It's Sunday, and my mother is at the church all day to help with the many services on Sundays. It's one in the afternoon, so I know they're wrapping up the noon service and won't have anything to do till the 6PM service. I went with her to the morning one, the 7AM service with all the true devotees. She makes me go so I figure I might as well go early and get it done.

I'm just sitting on the back porch staring off into the distance when Talus Fairneau pops into existence next to the back hedges. He appears as a human again today, but I still see through the illusion. He's only using it to keep prying eyes off him. Though, come to think of it, I wonder what my neighbors would think if they saw a middle-aged man in our backyard alone with me. Probably nothing good.

He comes up to me on the porch and I stand to greet him. He looks around in interest at my backyard and the house, taking it all in.

"You want a tour?" I ask him.

"Sure!" he says. "I've never seen an Earth dwelling before."

I grin at his enthusiasm and lead him inside. I show him around the downstairs, diligently showing him each room and explaining what they're used for. Then I take him upstairs, and he studies my room like it's a museum piece. I stand in the doorway watching him peer at my books and my posters on the walls and touch my bedspread to feel its softness.

"We don't sleep on beds," he says. "We sleep on the ground."

"You can test it out if you want," I say.

"Really?" he asks.

"Go ahead." I gesture for him to do so.

Talus Fairneau lays down on my bed, his head hitting my pillow. He shimmies for a moment, trying to get comfortable, and then settles down. A minute passes. "I *like* this," he says. "Why don't *we* do this?"

I laugh. "There's nothing stopping you from bringing a little human culture back to your homeworld."

"Nothing at all." He sits up and then stands up heading towards me. "I have to get one of these beds."

"You should!" He's such an odd character that I like him.

We head downstairs and outside again. I generally don't teleport inside the house, which is what got me in trouble with Lucy, but Ikthiel of course doesn't pay attention to that rule. So he often pops into and out of my bedroom on a regular basis. But I'm not going to do that with Talus Fairneau, because I don't feel like I should.

"You ready?" Talus Fairneau asks me as we stand on my back porch.

I check that my backpack is secure and then I nod and say, "Yes I am."

He holds out his hand and I take it, bracing myself for the inevitable jump. He tessers.

We reappear in the next second in the next galaxy. I bend over and heave, breathing deeply to keep from throwing up my breakfast. Talus Fairneau waits while I heave and try to calm my body back down. I doubt I'll ever get used to tessering. I'm amazed I haven't had a negative reaction to instantaneous travel before. The best I can do is just breathe through it.

Finally, I straighten up and look the professor over. He gives me a wan smile, his human facade having fallen away in transit now that he no longer needs it. His blue skin reflects the night sky around us making me look up and take in my surroundings.

My breath leaves me as I look at the view of the Milky Way galaxy hanging in space above us. It's so glorious and awe-inspiring and *home*. I smile up at it and think to myself how different our lives would have been if we grew up living in the Magellanic Clouds instead of in a central-ish arm of the Milky Way. How different we would be if we grew up with that view over our heads every night.

"It is breathtaking," Talus Fairneau says, bringing me back to the present.

"It is," I agree.

Around us on this rocky night landscape, boulders litter the sandy ground, ground that gives under my boots. In the distance rocky mountains cut a dark line against the galaxy. There is no vegetation, no animals, no people. There is nothing, just the rocks and the sand and the mountains. And us.

"Where are we?" I ask.

"Plesias Five," he answers, as if that means anything to me. In response to my blank stare, he adds, "It's a small planet in an old solar system." Again, that means nothing to me.

"So what are we doing here?"

Talus Fairneau smiles. "We're chasing a lead," he says. "I found a tiny reference to one of the Weapons being seen in proximity to your Milky Way galaxy. This seems a likely spot given that those boulders over there?" He gestures in the direction of the large boulders to our right.

"Yeah?"

"They're made of old matter, the kind we were collecting from Earth," he says.

My jaw drops. "There's pieces of it that are still that large?" I ask.

"Of course," he says, as if it's obvious there would be. "There's just a lot more matter that *isn't* old matter. And there certainly is a lot that isn't imbued with the original magic."

A thought occurs to me. "Can't we make new Weapons out of matter like this?"

Talus Fairneau shrugs. "I'm not sure," he says. "There's a technique to it that has been lost to time. And I'm not even sure the kind of beings that created the Weapons even exist in our modern universe."

"Weird," I remark, thinking that the universe is *less* diverse these days compared to earlier in time.

"Very," he agrees. "It's as if something was possible at the beginning of time that isn't possible now."

We start walking towards the boulder as we chat.

"What happens if we can't find the Weapons?" I ask, thinking dark thoughts about the reality facing all Witches, and really the whole universe. The Kolvat are a scary enough thought without considering this new potential threat Ikthiel brought to my attention.

"Well, then we're back to the beginning," he says. "The good thing is we're not the only ones searching for old Weapons or old spells that might work on the Kolvat."

"Or the other thing," I mutter under my breath.

"We are just the ones crazy enough to try and find the original Weapons," he concludes as if he didn't hear me.

We get to a particularly large boulder, one the size of a car perhaps, and Talus Fairneau lays a bare hand on the cold surface. Upon closer inspection, I realize he is wearing a shield of some kind around his hand, one that allows him to touch it while keeping the cold out. I am envious. My personal atmosphere kicked in when we got here, but it doesn't give me the ability to touch an object as cold as outer space.

He takes out one of his many devices and applies a small, circular blinking object to the boulder. It consists of one central light and what looks to be nine surrounding lights. I watch as the central light blinks on, and the surrounding ones follow suit. Each of the surrounding lights blinks in turn in a circular pattern that speeds up till I can't follow it anymore. I'm about to ask what the device does when my question is answered.

A spell matrix draws itself from the device, one that traces lines of golden light on the boulder surface. I watch as the lines completely enclose the boulder and reverberate in time with the blinking lights. The boulder shifts slightly in response.

"What are you doing?" I ask.

Talus Fairneau answers, "Asking the boulder where its friends are."

My eyebrows go up. Asking a *boulder* where its friends are? That idea feels ludicrous and yet here we are proving the idea to be a solid plan. The spell matrix puts up an energy screen with words spelling out in the common alphabet. I watch and read the words as they appear.

Nearby.

After the lone word, several sets of coordinates spew out, all of them probably translated from the boulder's sense of direction. I can't believe I'm thinking about a boulder having a sense of direction, but here we are. On a barren planet. Talking to a boulder.

The list of locations goes on and on.

"I think we need to be more specific," Talus Fairneau says. He taps the screen, and a question appears on it asking if there are any like it carrying power, shaped by magic, in the near quadrant. For a solid minute, the display stops spewing words. Then it gives its short reply.

One.

And the set of coordinates is short and sweet following the loan word. My stomach flips. Did we really just find the location of a Weapon?

Talus Fairneau thanks the boulder, a concept I'm still struggling with, and closes out the device causing the spell matrix to disappear. He puts the device away.

"What now?"

"We go find it," he says.

"I don't understand the coordinates," I admit. "Where is it?"

Talus Fairneau looks over at me in amusement. "It wouldn't make sense to most people as it uses me as the center and gives a position relative to where I'm standing," he explains. "The Weapon, if it is indeed one, is in your galaxy's halo. In a globular cluster on the other side from here."

My stomach drops. The jump is going to be a long one, all the way through the Milky Way and beyond.

"Shall we?" he asks, extending a hand to me. It's the first time I note that his hand, his real hand, has only three fingers.

I gulp and take a deep breath. Then I take his hand.

Talus Fairneau tessers.

17

June 26

Lucy

It's almost four by the time I make up my mind. Stewing for a week doesn't sit well with me. I want to go talk to Penny. I don't know what I'm going to say. I have no idea how I really feel. And I have questions that only she can answer. Questions about her power, her life, her choices, and the people who seem important to her. I want to know more.

So I sit there giving myself a pep talk in my bedroom, trying to keep myself from chickening out. It's only four o'clock. She's probably home. There's no reason I should wait any longer. I can go now and get this whole thing cleared up right now. I need to try.

Or not.

The doubt keeps creeping back in. I can't seem to push the thoughts from my head. I can't keep the doubt quiet. I'm really hurt by all this, by everything she kept from me. And I don't think I've forgiven her yet. But that's only going to come with time.

I hear the doorbell downstairs.

I look out my window and see Bryce standing on the porch. He's probably come to talk me into going to talk to her, like he has for the past week. It's getting annoying but it's understandable. I probably need the prodding.

A few minutes later Bryce knocks on my bedroom door. I tell

him to come in. He opens the door and shuts it softly before sitting on the bed opposite me.

"Hi," I say.

"Hi," he answers. "What's going on?"

I sigh emphatically. "I'm working up the courage to go over to Penny's house," I answer truthfully. He can see right through me so there's no point in hiding what I'm thinking.

"Good!" he says.

"Not good," I answer. "I can't seem to work up the courage to do it."

"You want me to come with you?" he asks gently.

Suddenly the monumental task of going over there feels much smaller. It feels attainable. "Would you?" I ask.

"Of course!" He reaches out and takes my hand. "I'll help you with anything."

I smile wanly. I don't feel worthy of that kind of affection right now.

"When are you thinking of going over?" he asks.

I shrug. "I was gonna try to go this afternoon, but it's already almost four thirty," I explain.

"Excuses," he says. "Let's go over. Now. While you're ready and I'm here."

He gets up from my bed and pulls me to my feet. I go to my closet and pull out some shoes, put them on, and then stand there with my shoulders slumped in utter defeat. "Do I have to?" I grumble.

"Yes," he says sternly. "It's time."

I sigh again. I feel like I'm sighing a lot these days. "Fine," I mutter.

I lead him out my bedroom door and through my house. I yell to my mother that we're going to Penny's, and she's so engrossed in her work she barely acknowledges it. I shut the front door.

We walk down the sidewalk, on the usual route to Penny's house. Only this time it feels like the walk takes forever and we aren't going to get there anytime soon. When we turn the final corner, the same corner I saw her and Altair from, I see her mother's car is missing from the driveway. Right. It's Sunday.

"Maybe she's not home?" I ask.

Bryce knits his eyebrows. "We should knock."

So we head up the front walk to her house and knock on the door. A few minutes pass. I knock again. No answer.

"Her mom's probably still at the church," I say, thinking out loud. "She might be there."

"Your mom could drive us?" he asks. Neither of us has more than a learner's permit yet.

"Maybe," I say slowly. She seemed distracted when we left, but maybe we could get her to do it.

I should take this as a sign that I'm not meant to talk to her today. I huff in annoyance.

"Let's go," he says. "If she's at the church, then we can catch a ride home with her mom."

"Sure," I say slowly. Her mom is weird and makes me uncomfortable, but she's technically a responsible adult. So I guess we could get home that way.

We head down the street and back in the direction of home. By the time we get back to the house, I'm sweating from the heat. The cool air conditioning is a relief after the outside air. Bryce shuts the door behind us, and we head to my mother's office. I tap on the doorframe to get her attention. She looks up from her computer and whatever taxonomic conundrum she's working on and takes off her reading glasses.

"What's going on?" she asks.

"Can you drive us to Penny's church?" I ask. "She's not home, but I think her mom might be there and Penny might be too."

My mother blinks at our question and knits her eyebrows together. I can see her analyzing all the reasons why we need to go to the church and talk to Penny *right now*. I can't think of a single logical reason that would make sense and also not be the truth.

Bryce jumps in. "We have an assignment due this week and she's not answering her phone," he says smoothly. I'm impressed.

"Oh," my mother answers taken aback. "I can take you. Are you going to be there long?"

"We can get a ride home from Penny's mom," I volunteer.

My mother's eyebrows furrow at that remark, but she keeps her thoughts to herself. "Alright, let me get my purse," she says.

Grateful that she didn't press any further and that Bryce thought of a solution, I let out a tight breath once she's out of earshot. That's part of this whole thing that is getting to me. Penny is not only a liar, but she's turned me into a liar too. I would have happily volunteered the information to my mother if it weren't something so private, so sensitive. But there's nothing that can be done. I can't reveal Penny's secrets which makes me a liar by omission.

Bryce rubs my shoulder as we wait in the foyer for my mom to be ready to go. He looks at me sympathetically as if he knows how I feel. I shake my head in annoyance.

"Ready?" my mom says coming around the corner.

We head for her SUV and pile in. Bryce sits in the back as I take shotgun. About a ten-minute drive later, we've pulled into the parking lot of the church Penny's mom goes to and works at. She pulls around the back to the office door and stops.

"Are you sure you'll get a ride home with them?" she asks, seemingly skeptical of the situation.

"Yeah, no problem," I answer, desperately wanting her to leave without asking any more questions. That's the problem with my parents being scientists: they ask too many questions.

"Ok," she relents. "Be careful," she says, though I don't know how you could be otherwise in a church.

Bryce and I get out and wait for her to pull away. Once she's left the parking lot, we turn to the office door and head inside. The place is much as it was the last time we came here all those months ago, but this time there's a few people working. It's a busy Sunday afternoon and there's another service this evening. It makes sense for there to be more people here. It does complicate things though. It means more witnesses.

"Lucy? Bryce?" Penny's mom greets us. "What are you doing here?" She gets up from behind her desk, and I suddenly feel underdressed in my shorts and a t-shirt.

"We're looking for Penny," I say quietly. We're within earshot of the other people in the room, an elderly woman and two middle-aged women all dressed for church and deeply engrossed in whatever paperwork is on their desks. All three of them looked up when we came in, but none of them acknowledged us beyond that.

"She's not here," Mrs. Williams says, her voice dropping. My stomach sinks. "She sent me a note," she continues, pulling out her phone. Even softer, she asks, "She told you right?"

I nod and whisper, "Yes."

"What about him?" she asks, indicating Bryce with a glance.

"Him too," I say.

Her mother nods, and she taps her phone a couple times. Then she shows me the screen.

Going offworld. Be back for dinner probably. Will message again if not.

Offworld. The word stands out as if it's written in red and not in black and white. My stomach turns over. Penny's not here. As in *really* not here.

"She hasn't said she wouldn't be home yet?"

Her mother shakes her head. "Not yet. So I'm expecting her back for dinner," she whispers. "Do you want to wait for her?"

Indecision grips me. On the one hand, I don't want to call my mother and ask for a ride home after all that. It would only raise suspicions. On the other hand, I don't really want to wait in Penny's mom's church until dinner time.

I glance at Bryce and his expression is impassive. He's going to let me make this decision. Big help, that one.

"Well, I guess we could wait," I answer after a few moments have passed.

"You'll have to sit through service at six," she says, putting her phone away.

I cringe. "Aren't we underdressed for that?"

Mrs. Williams snorts softly. "Trust me, you're not," she reassures us. "People dress all kinds of ways at our church. Just sit in the back and I can find you afterwards."

"What should we do now?" I ask.

She looks back at her desk and seems to consider for a moment. "Well, I have some filing you could do in the back room, if you don't mind," she says.

I look at Bryce and his expression remains unchanged. What am I supposed to say to that? Be rude and turn her down? Internally I sigh. "Sure, we can do that," I answer, volunteering Bryce along with myself.

She smiles at me kindly and heads back to her desk. I follow and take the stack of folders she loads us up with. Then she leads us into the room where Penny was studying back in November.

"Those files all go in these two cabinets," she explains pointing to two by the door. "It's alphabetical and the names are on the folders."

I glance down and notice the names are all surnames. These are parishioner files.

"Let me know if you have any questions," she says. "It shouldn't take you long."

I nod and thank her, for what I don't know. Not only are we going to have to sit through the service, but we've been given work to do as well. This did not go as planned.

Bryce whispers, "It could be worse. She could have made us go home and change."

I cringe at what my mother would say to that. She'd probably think I'd lost my mind. "Here's hoping Penny is there when Mrs. Williams takes us back," I whisper.

"Let's hope," Bryce whispers back.

We get started on our stack of folders and begin filing.

18

June 26

Penny

This place is weird. Weirder than any place I've been. It's a jungle again, but the plants are growing in loops up and down and all around us. If they're even plants. The colors are grotesque, putrid pink and purple mixed with forest green and a pallid gray. The ground feels soft and yielding under my boots. What is this place?

Above the night sky shows only blackness with some stars. It takes me a minute to realize the reason we're not seeing the galaxy turning overhead is because we're on the side of the planet that points *away* from the Milky Way. It's unnerving to think that there's nothing out there but an abyss of space until you run into another galaxy. It feels like being in a boat on the open ocean.

"Up this way," Talus Fairneau says, jogging me out of my thoughts.

I follow him up the hill. I can't really see anything besides this jungle, besides these alien trees. So I don't know what's ahead of us or behind us. Or what could be living out there.

"What would the Weapon be doing here?" I ask softly, not wanting to startle the native creatures.

He leads us through a particularly dense part of forest before answering. "I'm not sure, but there's old metal in a lot of these plants," he says, "according to my readings anyway."

"Really?" I say. I stop in my tracks and look up at the trees with new appreciation. We don't have anything like these on Earth. Not even banyan trees or dragon trees look this strange.

"Yes," he says. "There's metal in the wood."

I almost reach out to touch a tree but think better of it. I'm not fully shielded at the moment, and I don't need to come down with any kind of alien rash or whatever when I don't have immediate access to Witch medical care.

"This way," he says, studying his device.

We walk for what feels like miles but is only about a hundred yards. The hill slopes downward after a while and I find myself bending my knees to the point of crouching to keep from falling down. I don't want a repeat of Nahnu-beit out here where I don't know where Ikthiel is or if he can get to me.

"Here we go," Talus Fairneau says, leading us laterally along the side of the hill to what looks like a cave opening.

"It's in a cave?" I ask, thinking it's a little spot on.

"The cave is old, as old as the rock beneath the jungle," he says. "No doubt the magic in the Weapon kept the cave clear all these eons."

"Really?" I seem to be asking that a lot. Talus Fairneau has been an education. He knows much more than the readings he gave me and he's been open-handed sharing that knowledge with me. I appreciate it, but I constantly feel like I'm out of my depth.

"It's not uncommon on planets with low metallicity to have metals in their foliage," he explains. "It tends to get picked up by what's living."

He conjures a Witch light with ease and glances back at me. It takes me a second to realize he wants me to produce one too. Luckily this is a piece of magic I actually know. I produce the little spark of blueish yellow light that most Witches produce. It always feels nice to have something "normal" about my magic for once.

"Let's take it slow," he says, leading us into the cave.

The opening is the size of a school bus and twice as tall. As we go in, the dim light of the planet slowly seeps away as we enter the dark. One long walk down into the dark and the cave opens up into a cavern almost perfectly oval in shape. Talus Fairneau tosses his light out into the central part, instructing it to float in midair and brighten. The light shines on the walls of the oval cavern, showing carvings and markings that definitely aren't natural. This place was made.

"Is this what you were expecting?" I whisper, for some reason unwilling to speak loudly in here.

"No," he whispers back, the bluish light from his Witch light illuminating the concern on his face. "Look," he says. I follow his gaze.

There at the center of the room, floating in midair, is what we've been seeking. From what I can tell, it's shaped like a long-handled ax or hammer. Like a sledgehammer almost in design. I can't make out the details from our vantage point.

"How do we get it?" I ask. The floor between us and the Weapon is equally as carved as the walls and the ceiling. I'm not sure walking on it is a good idea.

"Perhaps we float," he says. "Or we ask it to come with us."

The Hammer begins to glow with his words. The dull gray metal suddenly gives off a radiant light, a greenish, grayish, purplish luminescence that lights up the whole of the cave. All around us the carvings on the walls light up as well, as if we tripped some alarm on this place.

"Don't move," Talus Fairneau advises.

I take his advice.

The lines of light near our feet begin to seep closer to us. Before long the lines surround us and begin to creep up our legs. I would be freaked out if not for the warm, oddly comforting sensation of the lights. This is familiar somehow. It's a kind of spell matrix and it seems to recognize us as Witches.

I hold out my hand as the light circles my arms and round my head. I look down and see it swirling around me, finding every nook and cranny of my body and even tickling my ears. Next to me Talus Fairneau is the same: completely covered in light.

Just as spontaneously as it began, the light recedes. The matrix quiets to a dull radiance, and the Hammer sits waiting in the center.

"Does that mean we pass?" I ask softly.

"I don't know."

He takes two steps forward onto the spell matrix. The light glows brighter around his feet. He gestures me forward. I take my place next to him, my feet also producing a steady glow. I feel welcomed somehow. Like an old friend asked us to be here.

Together we walk forward at a steady place, crossing the ten yards or so to the middle of the cave. The hammer hangs before us, only about five feet off the ground. I could even reach up and grab it. But I don't. That feels rude somehow.

"What now?" I whisper.

"We tell it what we need it for, I think," he says, reading his sensor. "There is some intelligence behind this place, behind the weapon." He tucks his sensing device away. "I think it needs to know we're not going to abuse its power."

Talus Fairneau reaches for the Weapon.

It immediately moves higher.

"It doesn't know about the Kolvat or the other thing," I say.

"You know about the other thing?" he asks.

I nod at him. I think I can trust him with my knowledge. "Ikthiel told me."

He nods as if that's not surprising. To anyone who knows me and knows my relationship with Ikthiel, it probably isn't. "Why don't you try talking to it," he suggests. "It recoiled from me."

I nod and look up at the Hammer. Up close it can only be described as a hammer. Definitely akin to a sledgehammer. I doubt it's that indelicate.

"We need your help," I say. "There's a threat to the universe out there. Two of them. We think you can help."

The Hammer doesn't budge.

"It's the Kolvat. They eat away at the physical world, as physical things," I explain. "They killed Widdershin, the planet of Witches. And they killed many other planets." I swallow, pushing my choked-up feelings aside for the moment. "And there's something else. We don't know what it is, but it's eating space. It's causing the universe pain." I know, somehow, that I'm speaking the truth. That somehow, someway the universe is in pain.

The glow from the Hammer brightens slightly. Then slowly, inch by inch, it lowers itself to my eye level. Not Talus Fairneau's eye level. Mine. I reach for it, and it floats into my hand. The hammer is cold to the touch but not so cold that I can't touch it. It stops glowing at my touch and stops hanging in midair, so I take the weight of it. It's top heavy and feels about the weight of a sledgehammer. I put both hands on it and cradle it to my arms. I hug the solid metal to my body and hold onto it. Upon closer inspection, the hammerhead has hexagons on either end of the column. I forget what that shape is called, but I'll probably search for it when I get home.

"What do we do now?" I whisper.

Talus Fairneau tries to take the Hammer from me, but it glows a dark red as his hand comes closer. He pulls his hand back. "Are you comfortable carrying it?" he asks. "It's not too heavy or anything?"

"It's not bad," I answer.

"I'm going to tesser you home," he says. "We'll take it to the Witches' War Council in a couple days."

I nod in agreement. "You want me to hang onto it?"

"Well, it won't let me touch it," he remarks. "You better keep it safe."

"I will," I promise. And I do mean it. It's one of the rarest things in our universe. How can I not keep it safe?

Together we walk out of the cave and back into the dim light of the strange planet. For a moment I feel like we're being watched, like the Hammer is being observed somehow. Maybe it's the trees. I don't know.

Talus Fairneau offers me his hand and I take it. He tessers us. I blink, and we're in the backyard of my home. It's dark outside, and my stomach sinks, thinking about how late it is and that I'm home after dinner. Then I notice my stomach didn't heave for once. It confuses me not to be bent over feeling sick.

I let go of Talus Fairneau's hand. "Thank you," I say cordially.

"You're not sick," he remarks.

"I guess not," I answer.

"Maybe the Hammer helps," he suggests. "In any case, keep it safe. I'll see you in two universal days."

I'm glad he specified which kind of days. I wouldn't see him for a week or so then.

He bids farewell and then disappears, his tesseract snapping him into another far reach of the universe.

I smile to myself as I look up at the stars. For once the smile feels natural. I turn and head into the house. I step inside, into the space between the kitchen and dining area and freeze.

Lucy and Bryce are sitting at the table eating dinner with my mom.

My heart pounds in my chest and I grip the Hammer tighter.

"There you are," my mother says. "Do you want dinner?"
I honestly don't know what to say.

19

June 26

Penny

I swallow, staring at Lucy and Bryce. I hadn't seen either of them in over a week. I was convinced she still hates me. And here I am standing in my kitchen holding the Hammer with my backpack still on and everything with Lucy and Bryce sitting at the table with my mother. Could this be more bizarre?

"Penny?" my mother asks.

"Huh, what?"

"Do you want dinner?"

"Yes, thank you," I answer. "I'll just go put this . . . away."

And I scurry out of the room and up to my bedroom without stopping. I carefully set the Hammer down on my bed and pat it softly to tell it that it's going to be alright. The Hammer glows briefly then goes quiet as if it's ok with that assessment. Weapons. With personalities. I can't handle this right now.

I drop my backpack and take off my boots. I realize then I tracked some dirt from the other world into the house. Oh well. Extraterrestrial dirt is now on my list of things to clean up. I head back downstairs stopping at the bottom to breathe for a moment. Then I round the corner, and my mother is standing in the kitchen handing me a plate of meatloaf with broccoli and mashed potatoes. I take it and sit down at the end of the table, looking at Bryce and Lucy on either side. My mother sits down at the other end of the table facing me. I have no idea what's going on.

"Lucy and Bryce came to the church to find you," my mother explains. "They stayed and helped with filing. The least I could do was repay them with dinner."

Lucy gives me an awkward smile. I really don't know what to say.

"So, how was your trip?" my mother asks casually.

My jaw drops. "It was . . . ok," I stammer out. "We went far."

"Where did you go?" she asks casually as if she asks me this every time. I mean, she does, but not in front of guests. This is weird. Weirder than that planet I was just on.

"Uh, well, I don't know their names," I admit, my brain finally chugging back to life. "It was this barren planet in one of the Magellanic Clouds and this other jungle-type planet in a globular cluster."

My mother blinks.

"Oh," I say. "Different galaxy and one at the far edges of ours."

She nods, clearly taken aback by my descriptions, but she's hiding it moderately well. Lucy and Bryce simply stare at me. I have no idea how to handle this. I feel so awkward and embarrassed.

"What were you doing? What was that . . . thing . . . you carried in?" Lucy asks tentatively.

"Oh, that's the Hammer," I say, naming it that even though I'm sure it has a proper name that's been lost to time. That makes me wonder, but I set that aside and focus. "It's an ancient Weapon from the beginning of time."

"A weapon?" my mother asks, raising an eyebrow.

"Just one word for it," I answer. "It's a Hammer." I shrug, trying to keep her from freaking out. It occurs to me then that I'll never really be able to *explain* everything to these three people. My experiences are so different from theirs that there's no way I can explain it. Unless . . . An idea springs to mind that I have to set aside for the moment. Now is not the time for it.

"Who made it?" Bryce asks, a logical question probably.

"I don't know," I admit. "Neither does Talus Fairneau, who I was with."

"Who's that?"

I smile wryly thinking of him. "He's a professor of sorts, an archeologist of Witch artifacts," I describe the man. "He's Xirlan, from . . . I'm not sure where his homeworld is actually." Now that the words are flowing, I realize how freeing it feels to be able to talk about this.

"Is he a Witch?" Lucy asks.

I nod enthusiastically. "Most of the people I work with are," I answer. "I was asked to work with him on this project, though I'm not sure why. Maybe it was purely academic."

"Like a summer project," Lucy suggests. Her eyes follow me with guarded interest. It's an olive branch, an offering of peace.

"I guess," I say. "Certainly feels like it." I want so badly for her to forgive me that she could have said the sky is green, and I would have agreed with her.

All she does is nod in understanding, and I don't say anything, waiting for a reply.

My mother interjects, "What is the Hammer for?"

I look at her. She is asking an unusual amount of questions this evening, and I don't even know how to handle it. "I'm not sure," I answer honestly. "It was made so long ago that no one really knows the intent behind its creation."

"Why are they having you hold onto it?" she asks.

I give a wry smile. "Because it wouldn't let Talus Fairneau touch it," I explain. "And I'm only holding it for a week or so till we can get it to the appropriate authorities."

My mother nods in understanding.

For a second I feel just how bizarre this dinner is. Just how strange this mix of people is. My ultra-conservative Christian mother, my best friend who is mad at me who is also the daughter of scientists, her boyfriend, and me. What a strange group. All we need is Ikthiel to complete the hattrick.

I eat my mashed potatoes in silence. My mother offers Lucy and Bryce some dessert—she made brownies this week for church and apparently there's some left over. She gets up to get it, gathering plates as she does so. Lucy gets up to help with the dishes. I finish my meatloaf quietly.

After we've all eaten brownies, my mother excuses herself to her alcove, where she works on stuff for the church. I never wanted to have a job like hers where she brings work home every night. But here I am, just like her in that way, bringing my magical work home with me every night.

"Can we go talk upstairs?" Lucy asks tentatively.

I nod and answer, "Yes of course."

We take our brownies and milk and head upstairs to my bedroom. I close the door to the bedroom. I move the Hammer to the floor and sit at the head of my bed. Lucy sits at the foot like she always does. And Bryce looks around for a moment curiously before sitting in my desk chair. I don't know where to go from here.

"I have questions," Lucy starts.

"I'm ready to answer whatever you want," I say. The words are genuine, but I feel exposed and self-conscious at the moment.

Lucy exchanges a glance with Bryce who nods at her in encouragement. Watching their interaction reminds me of my interactions with Ikthiel. No wonder people always assume Ikthiel and I are in a relationship. I don't know what we are, but we're not there.

She opens her mouth to start, then shuts it, then opens it again. Finally, she just asks, "Who is Ikthiel to you?"

Naturally that's the first question she asks.

I take a deep breath. "Well, besides being the reason I know Witches are real, he's a friend. A good one at that," I add.

"A demon is your friend?" she asks skeptically.

"You sound like most Witches." I chuckle to myself. "Most Witches don't like demons *because* they're demons."

She blinks and looks at Bryce. "You mean they're just prejudiced because of what he is?"

"Well, yes, but more because of the choices he made," I answer. "He was a Witch once. He chose to not use his Spark."

"Spark?" she questions. "Ah, what you said you almost used last year." Her eyes widen in shock. "Does that mean you're a demon now too?"

I laugh. "No, of course not," I say. "That was due to willing substitution. I'm not morally bound by that."

"Ok, so he's a demon who used to be a Witch who chose not to use his Witch power Spark thing?" she says slowly, working out the details.

"Correct."

"What about Altair?" She's wringing her hands, a characteristic sign of stress for her.

My mouth tilts into a crooked smile. I knew we would get to him and his explanation would be much more difficult. "He's not from here," I explain. "As in not from this universe. He has the ability to teleport across great distances and even from one universe to another. I have a spell matrix from him that lets me jump great distances too."

"So he can teleport," she says. She looks at Bryce who has a glint in his eye. I remember then how much of a sci fi nerd Bryce is and think that he must be loving this. "And that's where you went."

"We went to another part of the galaxy for fun," I say. "He's basically a year or so older than us, and he doesn't always listen to what he's supposed to do. He's not supposed to jump us all over the place with his power right now."

"Why?" she asks.

"Because it attracts the Kolvat—the creatures that attacked the Witch's planet last year," I answer. "I might have driven them out of the universe, but there's still some here, and they're still coming back in."

"That's concerning," she says, fully grasping the direness of the situation.

"Could they come here?" Bryce asks.

"Yes," I say truthfully. "Which is why I haven't been using my power. They don't seem to know where I am."

He relaxes a bit. "What about the Witches though?" he asks. "Why aren't you still out there learning?"

I sigh emphatically. "I really don't know," I say. "I am not exactly known for being easy to get along with. I have an attitude problem."

"Well, that's understandable," she says immediately.

My jaw drops.

"Well look at all you've been through!" she says, defending me. "I didn't know about your dad before, but I understand why you've been depressed and angry now. I understand where that comes from."

And just like that I'm reminded why Lucy is my friend. Just like that I feel how desperately I want her to be my best friend again.

"Can we be friends again?" I ask softly.

"Of course we can," she says. "But I don't want you to hide

anything from me. I want to know where you've gone and what you're doing. I want to be your friend again and I haven't been because I didn't know the whole story."

I swallow, thinking about all the betrayal she must have felt, but also about how she must have felt like she let herself down because of me. I have to make this up to her.

"Ok," I say. "I'll be truthful and open."

"Good," she says. "Because I have more questions."

"Proceed," I say with a wave of my hand.

I settle back on my bed and begin the arduous process of describing my life for Lucy and Bryce. And slowly, over the next hour or two, I begin to feel right again. Like I've been out of sorts for years and I'm now coming back to myself. By the time they get up to leave, they both have a much better sense of my situation and who I am to the Witches. And I have a better feeling about our friendship.

I shut the front door as they head down the street knowing my trust isn't misplaced. Knowing I've found the right friends to confide in.

INTERLUDE

Naymeth Nireson has walked many worlds. She has lived many lives, her life extending longer than many mortal creatures, her talent being for self-healing. She has lived so long that her Point of Importance has come not once but three times. She was able to do great things with her healing power keeping her intact. She lived so much that she found the oldest of things and the wisest of beings. She learned the names of those who are called gods.

This is the strangest task she has ever been given by those who would be gods, but she doesn't question their motives. The All-Seers tend to work in timelines of eons, not the breaths of mortal lives. She has seen more than one eon now and can't help but wonder when her time will come to an end here. She wonders if one day they will call her a god too.

This planet is young. It is a volcanic mess of lava flows and rocky promontories and acid rain in the night sky. She walks with a slight shield on, for though she can heal from all those things it does sometimes prove to be a nuisance to do so. She walks through the debris of the recent volcanic explosion, through the mountains on the planet's only continent, to the place that was selected. She had a hand in picking this place, but it was really the All-Seers who chose it.

"Why here?" she mutters to herself. The great hero of Vestrian folklore is also someone who talks to herself. She never feels like a hero. Not really, anyway.

This place feels unlikely and maybe that's why it was chosen. She hauls the Mallet with her, though it is light to the touch for her. The Mallet with its six-sided hammerhead and its long staff is slung across her back waiting to be placed in its home. It's home until the next worthy one comes to find it.

After what feels like hours, she comes to the place selected. She finds a stable place to stand and begins the spell. With elegant movements reminiscent of the water dancers of Lackanor, she begins to conduct the rock from its place. She begins to coax the rock free to build the cave where the Mallet will live untouched for eons. She may not live to see this place again, but she will make it a home for the Mallet. She will make sure it is something she is proud of.

By the time she is done conducting the rock from its home, she knows the cave is perfectly oval and waiting deep within the mountain. Satisfied and a bit tired from the exertion, she walks with her head held high into the cave. Her long, braided hair swings down her back, rubbing up against the Mallet which begins to illuminate in response. It lights up the cave for her.

When they get to the precipice of the oval cavern, she stops. There, she removes the Mallet from her back and sets it down carefully next to her. It stands on its own next, balanced on the end of the staff. She begins the next, harder part of the work.

Spell matrices are still relatively new to her, something invented a long time ago but only widely used recently. She builds one with tentative expertise, the raw lines of power cajoled into existence to form line after line of a sphere. She widens out the sphere until it forms an ellipsoid floating in the acidic air. Then she pushes the lines of power until they are embedded in the rock, digging and burning lines of power into the cavern walls.

No one would be able to enter this cavern who is not worthy of the Mallet. And the Mallet itself would have the choice. Naymeth is satisfied.

She takes the Mallet from her side and lifts it into the air.

"Goodbye, my friend," she whispers. The glow dims down in response, almost as if the Mallet is sad to see her go.

Even so, the Mallet takes its own weight and floats to the center of the room, between the two focal points of the spell matrix. She is ready to leave the Mallet behind.

With that task complete, she turns around and leaves the cave, not wanting to waste any time and ready to return to her duties. Once beyond the edge of the caves, she uses her transport device to teleport out.

What she doesn't see is the beginning of the changes of the planet. What she doesn't see is the calming of the lava and the stabilizing of the atmosphere and the eons of plants that grow long after. And she doesn't see the lone human and Xirlan come to her hiding place to retrieve the Mallet many eons later.

But she does see the incursion on the universe. And she sees what must be done.

PART 3

20

July 3

Penny

The day Talus Fairneau gets back in touch with me, I also get a message from Lucy asking to spend time together. The past week we've been around each other and talked and made light of the whole thing, but we haven't really had another in depth conversation. Her message sounds like that's what she wants.

I have the Hammer sitting across my crossed legs in my lap, keeping me company while I figure out what to say. The object isn't heavy with me, for some reason. But I haven't seen Ikthiel so he can judge it for himself. It feels like the Hammer changes depending on who is near and who is holding it. I've been taking notes on it for Talus Fairneau's benefit.

After an hour of waiting on a quiet Sunday afternoon, I finally answer Lucy back. This time I tell her the whole truth and don't leave out any details.

> **I have to meet with Talus Fairneau to return the Hammer to the Witches' War Council. I'll be offworld for at least the rest of the day.**

I send a similar message to my mother, noting that I'll message again if I can't make it home for dinner. It is only one in the afternoon right now. I'm already tired from going to church this morning.

My phone buzzes. It's my mother.

Dress warm. See you tonight or tomorrow.

And then a second message comes through from Lucy.

Can I come by tonight if you're back early enough? I want to ask some more questions, if that's ok.

I let out a tight breath. I can't promise to be home when I might not make it back. So I answer the best I can.

I'm not sure when I'll be back. But I'll message you when I am. I might not make it home tonight, if things take a while.

There's a pause for a few minutes, then the reply.

Kk. I'll be here. Just let me know. We could go to the beach for the 4th. If you could bring your fish friend, that would be cool.

I smile to myself. Lucy is predictable in one sense: fish. She's just fascinated with them.

I'll try to get Firrl out here sometime this month.

I'll have to keep that promise.

My phone doesn't buzz again so I put it on the charger to be left here while I'm offworld. I don't need to lose it on some random volcano or something. I'm always afraid it's going to break in transit.

From my wrist communicator, I shoot Talus Fairneau a message and ask where we're meeting the Witches' War Council. He tells me they're on a ship a few galaxies over right now and that it's cold in space. He tells me to dress warm. Why do these people not think I know how to dress for outer space? It's not like I didn't live there for a whole year and a half or so.

I put on my winter clothes again, my dark jeans and a long-sleeved top along with a black sweater. I grab my winter jacket that falls to my hips and provides adequate coverage before grabbing my combat boots. For some reason my mother was fine with those boots, and I wear them all the time. There's still dirt on them from when we got the Hammer. I pull on my boots and gather up my things into my backpack. I shove my laptop in there, thinking I might get one of the tech guys to upgrade it for me, and then throw in a change of clothes and some other miscellaneous stuff like a book I've been reading. Satisfied that I'm covered if I need to be gone till tomorrow, I zip up the bag and shoulder it.

I pick up the Hammer and think about how I would carry this long term if I had to. Probably across my back or something. Luckily, I don't have to carry it long term.

Downstairs I check that all the doors are locked, but that the chain is off the front door so my mom can get in when she gets home after church. To think it was only a week ago that I came home and found Lucy and Bryce having dinner with her after having attended service just so they could find me. Such a strange week it's been. I shut off most of the lights but leave the living room lights on just in case mom gets home late. I take off my backpack, put on my overcoat, and put my backpack back on.

A "pop" sound outside indicates Talus Fairneau is here.

I head out back and lock the door with my keys. I pocket my keys before joining Talus Fairneau on the lawn. He smiles at me and extends his hand.

"Are we jumping straight there?" I ask, hefting the Hammer and adjusting my backpack.

"Yes, straight onto the ship," he says. "They're traveling through the Dalus sector of the Oxrd arm."

I have no idea where that is. I just have to trust he knows where we're going.

"Ready?" he asks, his hand still extended.

I nod and take his hand.

Talus Fairneau tessers.

The ship pops into existence around us. Once again, I don't feel like throwing up. The Hammer in my hand provides stability to me, glowing softly, almost sympathetically. I let go of his hand and look around at the ship. We're in some sort of transport room with transit squares on the ground behind us. It looks like Talus Fairneau tessered us into a place where transits are normal. He is being polite.

"Talus Fairneau," he says to the transit controller.

The controller looks at me expectantly. Belatedly I realize he wants my name.

"Penelope Williams," I state.

The controller takes down our names in the database and glances up at me when he pulls up my file. He must have seen my power rating or something. He gives us clearance to board the ship, and I follow Talus Fairneau out of the transit room and down a hallway.

I quickly lose track of where we're going as he takes me through the bowels of the ship and to an elevator of sorts. We step onboard and he indicates on a panel where we're going. The elevator begins to move. It stops three times and people get on and off as needed. By the time we get to where we're going, six other aliens are riding with us.

We step off the elevator, three of those aliens following us, and head down a corridor straight away from the elevator doors. Every wall has a light up computer interface. Every hallway is lit by bright ambient light strips along the ceiling and the floor. The sleek design of the ship is so high tech I feel awkward and out of place in my Earth clothes. All I can do is keep up with Talus Fairneau and hope no one thinks me too weird as we pass by.

Down the corridor, to the left down another passage, and along a promenade that clearly runs along the exterior of the ship—it's windows distract me for a moment before I catch up to Talus Fairneau's rapid gait—and we arrive at the room we're apparently going to. The door doesn't open automatically as I've seen some of the others do. He pushes a button on the panel to the right of the door. From within the room, a tone reverberates so low I can barely hear it. The door smoothly slides open revealing an Ingtax beyond. They see us, register who we are and what I'm carrying, and wave us through.

Beyond the threshold, I find a dim interior. No doubt the lights ae low to accommodate the light display hovering in the center of the room. On that display is a location I don't recognize—not surprising given how big the universe is—with a giant red light in the center, tendrils coming off it. It takes me a moment to recognize that the shape of it is the Edge. It takes me a moment because the shape has a chunk taken out of it on one side. The thing eating away at spacetime has gotten larger than when Ikthiel showed me from his memories.

Talus Fairneau leads us into the room, and I find myself

surrounded by so many higher ups that I feel intimidated by the leadership in this room. The power in here rivals my own, but I know I edge them all out even if they combined all their forces at once. I might not have the experience this room has, but I do have the power. I raise my chin and stand taller to remind myself of who I am and what I'm carrying. The Hammer chose me after all. It didn't choose Talus Fairneau.

"You have it," a voice says from the dimness across the display. I can't make out who spoke, but it was definitely a woman.

"Yes," Talus Fairneau says, "Penelope carries it."

"May we see it, Miss Williams?" the voice asks.

The display collapses and winks out plunging the room into darkness. The ambient light slowly comes up, revealing the faces of those around me. There, across the group from me and clearly the one who spoke, stands Alicia Cole. I swallow, thinking about all the rules I've broken in the past two weeks. I feel a shiver of doubt run up my spine. Then I stand tall, almost haughtily, and raise my chin at her presence. I have the power here. I hold the Hammer.

I take a few steps forward and bring the Hammer to the center of the room. Alicia Cole comes forward. The Hammer glows reddish in response to her proximity and jerks away from her hand as she reaches for it. Affronted she reaches for it again. Again, it jerks away from her.

"It doesn't like you," I remark, perhaps not speaking the most tactfully.

"No," she says. "Someone else should try."

My stomach sinks. Part of me doesn't want to let go of the Hammer. I have a feeling if I let go of it now, I'll probably never see it again. But that's ridiculous because I have the power to use it. To power the damn thing with my strength.

Several other Witches come up to attempt to take the Hammer from me. They all fail until a little Speridrome female comes up and asks politely for the Hammer. The Hammer glows that distinctive blue showing its approval. I hand it to her, knowing she'll be able to carry it. She takes it with ease. I rejoin Talus Fairneau at the side of the room.

"Now that that's settled," Alicia Cole says, "let's get back to the issue at hand, shall we?" The annoyance in her voice is clear as day.

I clearly rubbed her the wrong way. I just hope that doesn't come back to bite me.

She continues, "Talus, what can you tell us about the Weapons and their usage?"

Talus Fairneau begins telling the story of the Weapons.

21

July 3

Penny

After about hour of speaking, Talus Fairneau has given a lengthy explanation of the Weapons and their mythology. Everything he told them was in my required reading. He declined to add his own research to the pile of knowledge, a fact that makes me wonder.

"Well, what do we *do* with it? And can it even stop the incursion?" one of the Witches asks.

I have no idea who anyone is besides Alicia Cole.

The argument begins and goes on for some time. But no one makes any significant points. Everyone is just shooting in the dark. I see why Ikthiel was insistent that no one knows what's going on. They have no clue how to handle this. They don't even have an idea about what it is exactly.

The lights dim and the display comes back up. They start arguing over that, over the obvious eating away of the universe by some outside force. I can't believe they're just arguing instead of trying to do something. *Trying to do what?* I have no idea what would work. I have no idea what would help this.

I shake my head slightly and watch the back and forth with mild annoyance. This is the kind of political game I hate. The kind of politics that keeps me on Earth and away from the war effort. And these are supposed to be some of our most seasoned and well-trained Witches. These are supposed to be people that can figure things out.

I feel once again how at a loss I am. I feel totally useless. I just stare at that malevolent roiling of the universe and watch as the Edge gets eaten away.

Then something clicks. I realize what I've been thinking for the past ten minutes, and it comes to the forefront. We keep saying that the universe is being *eaten away* at the Edge. What if that *exactly* what's happening? What if something is *eating* the universe?

But that can't be the case. It's coming from outside the universe. It's coming from someplace that doesn't exist.

Or does it?

My jaw drops as I realize that we've been thinking about this all wrong. We've gotten this so wrong I don't think we're going to come back from it if we don't try here, right now, to fix it.

I raise my hand like I'm in school. I don't feel weird about that because I am in school, but I feel weirdly young in this group.

No one recognizes me.

Frustrated at being ignored again, I march into the center of the room where the display warps around me. In sheer annoyance I raise my voice saying, "Hey! I think you're all wrong!"

A shocked silence follows my words.

Then Alicia Cole is the one to speak. "You are out of line, Miss Williams," she says. "This is beyond your experience."

"No, it's not," I growl at her. "It's clearly beyond *all* of our experiences."

Alicia Cole lets out an exasperated sigh. "Do you have a point to make?"

"Yes," I answer angrily. "We're thinking about this problem all wrong. We keep describing it as something eating away at the universe. But what if that's exactly it?"

Skeptical murmurs fill the room. I'm not having it.

"Hey!" I say loudly enough to get their attention. "I'm not hearing any good ideas or any ideas at all coming from any of you. Why don't you hear my idea out?"

The murmuring dies down. They know I'm right but they're not happy about it.

"So what exactly are you saying, Miss Williams?" Alicia Cole drawls out. She acts as if she is bored and annoyed by me. She probably is.

"I'm suggesting we're looking for the wrong culprit."

Silence.

"You're going to have to explain your reasoning a bit," one of the Witches says. I glance back at Talus Fairneau who nods encouragingly. At least someone believes in me.

"Alright," I say, swallowing my discomfort at being the center of attention. How do I describe this?

I think for a moment. An idea comes to me and as ridiculous as it is, I choose to go with it.

"Imagine you are a cell," I say. "But not just any cell, you're the cell of an apple, right near the core."

"Ok . . ." Alicia Cole drawls.

"You're following? I don't know if you have apples," I add to the rest of the room.

"We're following," someone says, amusement in their voice.

I nod. "So, you are a cell in the center of an apple, and the apple is your whole universe. And maybe you are the kind of cell that can move around and explore the apple, but you can never leave it. There's just you and the apple." I know I'm on a wild metaphor, but I can't help myself now. "And maybe you were there from the beginning or maybe you know that at the beginning, the apple was really a flower, and you became a fruit, and you're still not a ripe fruit yet—"

"Alright, we get it," someone grumbles.

"Good," I say unperturbed. "Now imagine you learn, after all this time, that there are other apples on the tree."

Alicia Cole's eyebrows go up, following my crazy metaphor. "You might want to learn how to jump from one apple to the next," she says. I *know* she is thinking of Altair.

"Exactly. You might move between apples, or communicate with other apples, or just generally realize that yours isn't the only apple that exists," I say, my old bitterness quiet for this moment. I always think of my parents when I think about things like that.

"Alright, so this is just another apple?" one of the Witches asks.

"No," I answer. "Stay with me." I realize I've been gesturing emphatically this whole time and for a split second I am self-conscious. Then I toss that aside and continue. "So, you and your other apple buddies are all just cruising along being apple cells and enjoying your apple existence when—*WHAM!*" I clap my hands together.

"*What?*" someone says, startled.

"A horse eats you."

"Are you saying the universe is being eaten by a horse?" Alicia Cole says sarcastically. Her tone of voice is one thing, but when I glance at her, I see in her eyes that she understands where I'm going with this. Out of everyone's line of sight but mine, I see her nod once. Maybe she isn't totally mad at me.

"Metaphorically, yes," I answer. "Up till this point we've assumed that all things must live *within* the universes. But if there's one thing the Kolvat should have taught us, it's how wrong that assumption is. So, what if the Kolvat are little creatures in a vast place of inter-universe-dwelling creatures?"

I see Alicia raise her eyebrows and answer, "You mean, what if the Kolvat are the birds, and we should really be worried about the horse?"

"Exactly." By some miracle I have managed to communicate my point.

"So what do we do about it?" This next question I expected.

"I have no idea," I say. The truth. "I was hoping someone might have an idea or two."

A murmur circulates the room, both amused and disturbed.

Alicia Cole takes the center of the room, and I am free to step back.

"Well, what Miss Williams has given us is the critical point: How do we become unappetizing to a horse?"

"Can you reason with a Universe-Eater?" a voice calls out. And just like that we have a name for the thing that is killing our universe. A Universe-Eater.

There is no response to the question posed. There is nothing but silence, a tense silence that speaks volumes. We have no clue how to defeat this thing.

"Miss Williams," Alicia Cole says, "Talus Fairneau, thank you both for retrieving the Weapon."

"It's a Hammer," I correct her.

"The Hammer," she says with a wry smile. "We will call you if we need you again."

Seeing that we're dismissed, Talus Fairneau leads us out of the room. In the corridor, we both pause and exchange a glance.

"Good insight in there," he says. "You're really learning to think outside of the normal boundaries."

I make a face. "I *am* outside of the normal boundaries," I say ruefully. "It would be sad if I didn't learn to think outside of them."

"True," he says. He leads me down the corridor back the way we came and to the elevator. We wait for it to come.

"Do you think they'll let me off of Earth after this?" I ask.

"I hope so," he says. "We could honestly use your power out there."

I clench my jaw. "That's what I feel."

"Give it time," he says. "And if that doesn't work, then make the decision for them."

"Make it for them?"

"Stand up to them like you just did to Alicia Cole," Talus Fairneau says. "You're so powerful, they're scared to upset you. Use that to your advantage."

"That feels like cheating," I grumble.

"So cheat," he says. "It's wrong that they're keeping you out there. You should be here, helping. Fighting for the universe."

I look up at him as the elevator comes to us. "You really think so?"

"I don't lie," he says as we step into the elevator with the four other people already in there. He punches a button to indicate where we're going. "In the meantime, let's get you home."

"Already?" I ask, disappointment saturating my feelings.

"Already," he says, with some regret. "But I'll come get you soon. We have more work to do."

I face forward in the elevator and shove my feelings of neglect aside. I feel like I'm being cast off again. Maybe Talus Fairneau doesn't realize it, but he's doing it too. My idea was taken, and then I was dismissed like the child I am. I'm not really a child anymore. I've seen too much.

Determination sets in. I feel the anger in my heart; the anger that had started to subside but still festers below the surface. I would *not* be cast off like this. I will not be set aside and made to do small tasks like I am not worthy of attention. I will find a way off Earth again. I will return to where I belong.

22

July 4

Lucy

I got Penny's text late at night saying she just got home. There was no way my parents were going to let me go over there at almost one in the morning. So I texted her telling her I would talk to her in the morning. I wanted to see her face to face, because some of the questions I have aren't the kind I would ask over text. So it would wait a day. I didn't sleep well thinking about my questions.

The following morning, I walk over to her house and knock on her door not knowing who to expect.

Her mother answers, "Oh hi, Lucy." She opens the door wider and lets me in. "Penny is still asleep from her trip last night."

"Yeah, I saw she got back late," I answer, coming in. "Can I go wake her up?"

"Please do," her mother says. "It's after ten o'clock."

So I head up the stairs to Lucy's bedroom, knocking on the door before bursting in.

"What that h——?" she says sitting up in her bed. Her hair is a tangled mess, and she looks genuinely startled. I almost regret waking her. Almost.

"It's after ten o'clock," I say. "You should be awake by now."

She grumbles and flops back down in bed, pulling the covers over her head. I walk up to her bed and tug on her foot.

"Stop it," she grumbles. "I had a long night."

"So I gathered," I answer. I shut her bedroom door and perch at the end of her bed.

She pulls the covers down and glares at me. "You're not leaving, are you?" she asks.

"Nope," I answer.

She moans dramatically. "Fine," she says. "Give me a minute." Penny extracts herself from her covers and heads into the bathroom. She comes back looking more refreshed and sits at the head of the bed, pulling her blankets around her waist. "You wanted to talk?" she asks.

"I wanted to ask you some questions without Bryce here," I answer.

"Oh?"

"Yeah, some girl stuff," I say for lack of a better term.

"'Girl stuff'," she repeats.

"Something like that," I answer. I pause. I'm not sure how to ask these questions of her. "It's about Ikthiel."

"What about him?" she asks, her eyes going wide. I can see the wheels turning in her head trying to figure out what I'm going to say next.

"Do you like him or something?" I plunge forward.

She narrows her eyes and asks, "Why do you want to know?"

I tilt my head, narrowing one eye back at her. "Why are you dodging the question?" I retort.

She snorts. "I'm not dodging the question," she says.

"Sure, you aren't," I answer. "You both looked really cozy with each other when we met him a couple weeks ago."

Her cheeks blush, which is more of an answer than she's giving. She looks at me like a deer in headlights, probably not having expected this line of questioning.

"We're not a thing," she says.

"Sure, sure," I say. I'm enjoying torturing her.

"What else do you to want to know?" she asks, annoyed.

"Oh, no, uh uh," I say. "We're not changing the subject. I want to know details."

"He's a demon," she says, as if that would answer everything.

"You described him as 'close' to you," I persist.

"I'm close to . . . people," she stammers out.

"No, you aren't," I answer, getting annoyed now. "You're close to like one person, and that's him. He probably knows you better than I do."

She gives me a rueful face. "Well, he can read my mind, so that does help."

My jaw drops. "Can he read other minds?"

Her chin lifts a little bit. "Yes," she says. "He can read everyone."

"Well, *that* would've been nice to know!"

She cringes. "Sorry," she mutters.

"Stop apologizing, and just tell me stuff!" I say in exasperation. "I want to know about your relationship with him."

"Well . . . he's . . . I don't know," she says. "I don't know what we are. But we're at least friends. Close ones, at that. I trust him." The words just pour out of her, until she stops talking and just stares at me.

"You like him." It's not a question.

She shrugs, the blush spreading on her cheeks. She's avoiding my gaze. "I guess I do."

"You *know* you do," I accuse her. "It's obvious you like each other."

That catches her attention. She looks up at me in alarm. "You think it goes both ways?"

"Can't you just . . . I don't know . . . read his mind?" I tease her.

She scoffs. "I could, but I'm not very good at it. I feel like it's an invasion of privacy, but he's told me I could. So I don't know." She throws up her hands. "He's told me about himself, more each time he visits. I asked him to tell me everything."

"What did he tell you?"

She pauses. "I'm not sure I should tell you what he told me," she says. "It's private stuff."

"Ok, well, give me the broad strokes," I concede. It's fair that she doesn't spill all of Ikthiel's private stuff. It wouldn't be right.

Penny tilts her head to one side and thinks for a minute. Then she says, "Well, he was a Witch before, a human at that. He's old." She gives a slight smile, and I know he's got her. She's hooked on him. "He's like over a century old. His power keeps him young and alive."

"Like a vampire," I quip.

She gives a wry smile. "Something like that."

We fall into silence, a silence that feels companionable for the first time in weeks.

Then she asks, "Is there anything else you want to know? Or can we get some breakfast?"

"I'd like to know a little more about Altair," I admit. "I want to know how someone can come from another universe like that."

Penny laughs. "No one understands Altair's power," she says. "He came from a planet, much like ours in his universe. Their power is different from ours. It doesn't have a sparkpoint. They never get their power exhausted like we do."

This prompts my next question. "What is a sparkpoint exactly? You tried to explain that to me before, but I don't really understand."

She takes a deep breath and lets it out. I can see this is a difficult topic for her. So I wait for her to start.

"A sparkpoint is a time at which the Spark of power in each Witch finds its point of action," she begins. "The Spark has a purpose, or so the Witches believe. They believe there is a reason for every person's power, a reason they have it." She lets out another breath. "I thought I had found my sparkpoint last year, but it wasn't the right time."

I study her for a moment. "You said something about it being a 'willing substitution'," I prompt.

"Yes, the planet spared me by sacrificing herself," she says.

The explanation is barely sufficient. I can't understand it really. Perhaps that's the great divide between us now. I can't completely understand her experiences because I'm not a Witch. Understanding dawns on me. I get it now. I understand why she didn't talk to me about all this stuff before.

"How does that make you feel?" I ask, wanting to understand more.

She gives a wan smile. I can tell the answer to that already. Her face says it all. "I don't know," she says. "I spent all of this past year trying to cope with it. I just don't know how to feel."

I nod and do my best to show the sympathy I feel. It must have been difficult for her to cope with her sparkpoint not coming through. It must have been the reason why she was so out of sorts, when she came back last year. So much makes more sense with all this context.

"Is there anything I can do?" I ask her.

She shakes her head. "I'm ok right now," she answers. "Knowing I can come talk to you now is really helpful actually."

A few moments pass, and neither of us says anything. Then she asks, "Can we get breakfast now?"

I laugh. "I've already eaten but I could eat second breakfast."

"Let's go do that," she says. She climbs out of bed and heads into the bathroom with clothes to change.

I look around her room, at the odd decorations that I know her mother had a heavy hand in choosing. I also take in the weird spiky lamp and the one image of a raven that are most definitely Penny's taste. I wonder if she even really knows her own taste anymore; she's been so controlled by so many people over the past five years. It's a wonder she doesn't lose her mind.

She comes out of the bathroom dressed in shorts and a t-shirt, the most conservative version of that outfit one could find. She seems comfortable and happy in it, though I don't think pink is her color.

"Are you sure you're ok here?" I ask her, the other burning question in my repertoire.

Penny looks taken aback. "I think happiness evades me," she answers, "but I'm ok."

I look at her, taking in the details of my childhood best friend. "I wish I could help you out of this place," I whisper.

The look she gives me is a mixture of gratitude and resignation. "I wish you could too."

Then we take ourselves downstairs. Her mother is sitting in the living room reading. Penny leads us into the kitchen. She makes us eggs for breakfast, a skill I didn't know she had, and we sit at the dining table and eat it together in companionable silence. I don't think we've healed our relationship yet, but I feel like we're on the right track.

23

July 16

Penny

Ikthiel shows up again. just when I wonder when he will be coming back. I'm not surprised by his visit, but I am surprised it took so long. I'm sitting in my bedroom reading a paper on the mythos behind the Weapons assigned to me by Talus Fairneau. That's when Ikthiel chooses to pop into my bedroom.

I sit bolt upright when he shows up, not just startled but a little pissed.

"Where have you been?" I demand. After he bears his soul to me, he just disappears for two weeks? I thought he would have been back sooner.

He gives me a wry smile. "Did you miss me?"

I scoff. "Of course I did," I say. "But it's not that. It's the whole thing with Lucy. I needed your support."

He gives me a doubtful look. "Somehow, I don't think you needed me for that," he says. "You are strong enough on your own. I'll always be here when you need me most."

I purse my lips in response. I bite back the harsh words inside of me and let go of the anger for once. I don't want to be angry with Ikthiel. Not after he's been such a constant support to me over the years. No, I just want someone to be angry with because I'm still angry at myself.

"That's better," he says in response to my thoughts. "I knew you'd get there eventually."

I roll my eyes in response.

He sits down on my bed, and I put my laptop aside for now. I'll have to finish my required reading later. There's no shirking responsibilities, when the fate of the universe is on the line.

"So where *have* you been?" I ask.

A dark look crosses his face. "I had a meeting with my demon 'friends', as you call them."

My stomach sinks. Nothing good can come from Ikthiel associating with them. "What did they want?" I have a bad feeling about this.

"They want more of your power," he says matter-of-factly.

Bad feeling confirmed.

"Romora called us back and wanted to know why I haven't reported back recently," he explains.

My chest tightens in response. I know how scared he is of those demons, even if he doesn't admit it to me openly. Though, come to think of it, he might admit that now.

"You remember me telling you about them last year?" he asks. I nod. "Well, they're not happy. And when they're not happy, things tend to break."

"You want my power again."

"I can give them what I retained myself, but honestly another dose would be helpful. Just giving them something to bide our time would be helpful."

I make a face. "They'll never be satisfied until their source is gone," I say rather bluntly. "They'd rather I be dead, than helping the Witches."

Ikthiel looks like I slapped him. But he doesn't deny it. So I know it's the truth, and that he knows it too. They want me dead.

"Yes, well," he says, "I don't want it to come to that."

"I know *you* don't," I say. "I just don't believe that they will ever let it go."

He just stares at me, watching me. His non-answer is an answer.

"I'm not giving up my power again," I say. "I did it last time to save you. I refuse to be manipulated again to give power to people who will misuse it."

Ikthiel cringes. "You don't know what these demons are like.

They're not like the demons you've worked with," he implores me. "Waspira is ruthless. She's tiny but ruthless. Matchen and Gethryl will kill you without a second though. Romora is so old she has powers none of us know about. But not one of them compares to how terrifying Disperao is. He won't just kill you. He'll make it so you never existed. No one will remember you. And there's no coming back from that, like there is from death."

I flinch at his reminder, that I've cheated death once already. There's no telling whether I'll be able to cheat it again. Still, it's a low blow. I feel like he's telling me to do this. I feel like he wants me to do it. But I can't. Not again.

"What you just told me makes me less likely to give them my power," I state emphatically. "I didn't want to give them my power a year ago, and I don't want to now. Only this time I'm not going to."

"Are you sure about what you're doing?" he asks.

"What do you mean?"

"They're going to come after you, if they don't get what they want," he says. "I can only protect you so far. I can't take on five powerful demons. I'm not that powerful."

"I'm not asking you to protect me," I retort.

"Yes. You. Are," he says enunciating each word. "By putting yourself in danger, you're asking me to protect you, whether you say the words or not."

I blink. What is he saying?

"I'm not going to let anything happen to you, Penelope," he says. "If it's within my power to do so, I will protect you. Even if it *isn't* in my power, I'll still try."

My jaw clenches and unclenches. I just stare at him, watching him. Something has shifted between us. I don't know what exactly, but something is different. Our relationship changed with that proclamation.

Ikthiel swallows and reaches out to take my hand. I let him. His claws are the shortest I've ever seen them.

"I'm scared for you," he says. "I'm scared for us. None of them are to be trifled with, and they *will* come after both of us."

I tilt my head and look at him, study his features and the way he's being vulnerable with me. It begs the question though. "Are you scared for me or yourself?"

"Both," he admits openly. "I'm terrified of Disperao in particular. I think on a good day, I can probably handle the rest of them one-on-one. But him? He'd wipe us out of existence, before we had a chance to fire a single shot."

I swallow at the description. "Can he be stopped?"

"He's not invincible, but if he uses his primary power, he'll be nearly impossible to beat."

My stomach churns. "So he would use it, even though they need my power," I say.

"Yes."

"Well, that's terrifying." I swallow compulsively. I feel on the edge of deciding the other way and giving my power to them. What I concluded remains true though. If I give them more now, they'll only keep coming back until I'm exhausted or dead.

"You still won't," he says, a little begrudgingly.

"I still won't." I purse my lips, bracing myself for another fight.

But the fight doesn't come. He simply holds my hand and watches me before he says, "I respect your choice. I don't agree with it, but I respect it."

"Thank you," is all I can think of to say.

"I care about you, Penelope," he says. "I really don't want to see you hurt. And I certainly don't want to forget about you."

I nod at his words. "I care about you, too," I reply. "And I don't want anything to happen to you, either."

"I'm glad we're in agreement."

I squeeze his hand and then ask the final question. "What do we do about them? About the demons, I mean."

"I'm not sure," he says. "I will think about it and avoid them in the meantime."

"What if you can't avoid them?"

"Then I'll use the power you gave me and give it up completely," he says. "I'll use a drop to sate them for now, but I know it won't last."

"You think I'm right, then," the realization hits.

"I do," he says. "But I still think you should give them your power to avoid confrontation."

"I know," is all I can say. "I trust your judgment, and I trust you, but I *don't* trust *them*."

He lets go of my hand and leans forward. He places a hand on either side of my head and kisses my forehead. "Be careful," he says. "They don't know where you are precisely, but they could find you if they tried. They definitely know how to find me."

"So when we're together, we're more at risk."

"Yes," he says. "At least, *you're* more at risk." He swallows, still holding my head and looking at me closely. I can feel his breath on my face. "I can't protect you, if I'm not near you."

"I know."

"Do you know? Do you know how badly they scare me?"

"I do," I say. I push into his mind and say, *I know.*

Ikthiel nods in approval. *You can always reach me like this*, he says. *Even from across the universe.*

Startled, I ask, "Even that far?"

"Thought doesn't travel the same as anything else," he explains. "No one knows why, really. But thought transcends spacetime."

"Will you come, if I call?" I ask.

"Always."

I give him a wan smile. "Even across the universe."

"Yes," he says. "Even from another universe."

I nod. He kisses my forehead again and sits back down. We sit like that for a while, before he suggests we get some lunch. My mind still on our exchange, I agree, and we head downstairs. I know I won't shake the feeling that things are different between us. That things have changed. I won't shake that for the rest of my life.

24

August 4

Lucy

It's a sunny day at the beginning of August. The summer feels in high swing, and there is a kind of tension in the air. The kind of tension that signals big changes or things that might come next. It's that tension as the summer comes to its peak, when we feel like anything can happen.

Today is beach day. We're all going to the beach to spend some time relaxing, before we have to go back to school in the fall. It's been a few weeks since Penny and I started rebuilding our relationship. This trip is going to be us and Bryce. Penny's mom surprisingly agreed to take us there and take a day off from work. So we pile into her mom's sedan and head to the beach.

We head for Oceanview Beach on Jekyll Island. The whole car ride, I sat in the backseat with Bryce, enjoying the changing landscape as we headed through the marshes. By the time we get there, I felt as if I'd been transported to another world. A feeling I'm sure Penny gets to actually feel on a regular basis.

We unload from the car and walk towards the beach, heading down the boardwalk to an access point and then finding a spot on the sand to set ourselves up. Penny's mom brought with her a beach umbrella and sets to work anchoring it to the ground. Then we lay out beach blankets in the shade under the umbrella and unpack our beach things. Penny's mom passes around bottles of sparkling water with fruit flavor in it, and we all drink gratefully. Even at ten in the morning, it's already hot out here. The breeze from the ocean feels nice.

No one talks for the first twenty minutes. Everyone just watches the water and listens to the sound of the birds and the other people on the beach. It's not crowded this time of day, and I'm grateful for that. No need to experience the overwhelming number of tourists who come down here, spending the whole day. We'll be long gone before the lunchtime and afternoon crowds show up.

"Lucy? Did you hear me?" Bryce asks.

"Hm, what?" I say. I really didn't hear him.

"I asked if you want to take a walk," he says.

"Oh, yeah, let's go walk the beach," I answer. "Penny, you coming?"

She looks up, startled, her gaze tearing from the waters as mine had done. "Yeah, I'll come with you."

We all get up and dust the sand off ourselves. We're all in our bathing suits, Penny wearing a white crochet coverup that suits her and me with a sarong tied over my two-piece. Bryce is shirtless, a sight not unfamiliar to me, but he is turning slightly pink. I realize we might need to put on sunscreen, before we head down the beach. I grab the little tube of white cream and hand it to Bryce.

"What?" he says, looking down in confusion. "Oh." He slathers some sunscreen on before handing the tube to Penny who mimics his movements. I take the tube from her and do myself. We're ready to go.

"Be careful," Penny's mom says. "Don't go too far."

I don't know what she defines as too far when her daughter travels regularly to other worlds. I don't bother asking.

We walk barefoot down the beach, feeling the nice cooling breeze coming off the ocean and the sand between our toes. Bryce trails behind, giving Penny and me some space to talk, I think.

"Are we ok?" Penny asks.

I look at her, then out at the ocean. "I think we're ok now," I answer honestly. "We weren't for a while there."

"I know," she says. "That's why I asked." She pauses. "I'm sorry I couldn't get Firrl out to visit. She was too far away to make the trip."

A smile involuntarily curls my lips. "It's ok," I say. "Next time."

"Next time," she agrees. "She loves Earth because of all the water."

"I bet." I grin at the thought. "She probably would hate aquariums, though."

"I told her about them," she says. I look up in surprise. "I didn't want her to be shocked at the thought. She understood why we do them, to help people understand what they can't experience. She was saddened by the fact that some animals experience abuse, but she said darkness is everywhere, and you have to face it sometimes."

The words feel so real to me, so true. I can't imagine the kind of darkness Penny has faced in her life now. First, her parents. Her father beat her nearly to death and kicked her out of her house when he didn't succeed. Then she learns that some Witches betray their own kind and kill for those beliefs. And just when she's dealing with that, she faces those creatures she called the Kolvat, and the darkness they bring to the skies. I can't imagine the power she wields. I can't imagine the responsibility she has on her shoulders. I just can't imagine it.

"I'm glad we're friends again," she says softly. "It means a lot to be able to talk to you about everything I've been going through."

"I'm glad too," I answer.

It's a burden to take on her feelings, her pain. But it's a burden I'm willing to bear.

"How is Ikthiel?" I ask her.

She smiles involuntarily. "He's good," she says. "He was here two weeks ago. We talked a bunch."

"Do you think he loves you?" I ask her, feeling in my gut the truth, before I even ask.

She blushes. "I don't know," she says. "I know he cares about me and he wants to protect me. Is that the same thing?"

"Do you not know?"

"I don't know," she says. "I don't know love, really. Not with everything that happened."

I take her hand and stop her walking. "I love you, Penny. You're my best friend, and I care deeply about you," I say emphatically. "I know we had a bumpy road this past month, but that doesn't matter now. We're ok, now."

She smiles but the tears in her eyes tell me how much she's touched by what I said. I meant every word. I know she's been through it, and we've had a hard time, but she is important to me. I won't turn my back on her like some other people would. I wouldn't do that. I would never do what her parents did.

We keep walking for a while, until we're a good distance down the beach. Bryce is still behind us, splashing in the surf. He makes me smile with his childlike wonder. I feel lucky to have him in my life too.

The sun is starting to get high in the sky, casting short shadows under us all. It's got to be closer to eleven or even half past now. Penny walks to my left, looking over the dunes and watching the grasses wave in the breeze. I look out over the water again as we walk through the edge of the surf. My legs are damp from the ocean, and I love the feel of it.

I hear Penny's sharp intake of breath.

I look over at her and follow her gaze past where Bryce is standing. Bryce is backing towards us now. Penny throws an arm across me and steps between me and the figure that just appeared out of nowhere.

"Whatever you do, don't go near them," Penny whispers to me and Bryce. "Don't let them touch you."

"What is it?" I whisper back.

"A demon," she says. "A bad one." She lets out a tight breath and steps forward. "Are you Romora?"

"No, *I'm* Romora," a voice says from behind us. A second female stands there, emanating evil even to my human senses.

"*Sh—*," I hear Penny swear under her breath. Then she says, "Ikthiel, I need you."

Another demon appears to our left and another to our right. Finally, a fifth demon stands behind Romora, a dark calm figure whose eyes follow us maliciously.

With a soft popping sound, Ikthiel appears next to us. He immediately stands between Penny and Romora.

"Is that Disperao?" she whispers, indicating the one next to Romora.

"Yes," Ikthiel whispers back.

"*F—*." She goes pale. "We're in trouble."

"I *will* have your power, Penelope Williams," Romora says, raising her voice and largely ignoring Ikthiel.

"Look out!" he says a fraction of a second before the blast of power comes at us—

And stops just a foot short.

A glowing curtain shields us from the blast.

Then a second blast comes from behind.

This time a second shield lights up around us. I look at Penny, who is staring at Bryce. I look at Bryce, his hands held out in front of him.

Bryce is casting the shield.

My heart seizes. What just happened?

25

August 4
Penny
Bryce is a Witch.
What the—
Now's not the time, Ikthiel says. *Defend yourself.*

I raise a shield of my own and stand facing the small female who must be Waspira. Lucy is sandwiched between me and Bryce and Ikthiel, the only one truly powerless here.

Waspira blasts me with fire first, then ice. By some miracle, my shield holds. How are we going to get out of this? How are we going to defeat five demons hell bent on getting my power?

I watch as the demons creep closer, closing the circle around us. They're setting up for something, but *what?*

My breath comes in ragged gasps, as I pour my power into my shields. Then I feel it. I look left, and one of the two demons—Matchen or Gethryl, I have no idea which—has reached my shield. He's made contact with it and is siphoning off the power. The more I pour into it, the more I feel seeping out of me and into him. He is a demon who is capable of taking power away. No wonder Ikthiel warned me about them. No wonder he was so scared he wouldn't be able to protect me. They can just absorb my power and use it later.

"They're going to kill you for your power," Bryce says matter-of-factly.

"I *know*," I growl. What the hell does he think he's doing telling me what's going on? Who the hell is he even?

Defend yourself, Ikthiel reminds me once again.

My shield absorbs a blast from behind me, from Romora or Disperao. I don't know which blasted my shield, but it knocked me to the ground from the weight of the power. Either of them could have done it. I don't know which and that scares me even more.

Lucy yanks me to my feet and holds me up.

"You can do it," she whispers. I see in her eyes the terror she feels. The terror at being in the middle of a Witch fight with no way to defend herself. So I throw my power into her too. At the contact with my arm, I throw power into her to protect her. To shield her from any blows that might come her way. She's not a Witch and won't be able to wield it, but maybe it'll protect her.

Then I feel another blast, this one much worse than the last. I turn around and look at Ikthiel, who is shielding us from Romora and Disperao as best he can.

"Disperao?" I ask.

"Yes," he says raggedly. He is not doing well. I can see his power being drained as well. He has a lot of it too, but nowhere near as much as I do. We have only minutes.

I fire back.

I use the power I have and aim it at the demon draining us.

No use. The blast gets completely absorbed by his power.

Fine. If I can't take him out, I'll take out the other two.

So I turn my attention to Waspira and her firepower. I turn my gaze on her and think one angry thought. *Vanish.* And with the level of power coursing through me, the kind of power that I don't normally wield, that thought is all it takes. I feel her vaporize into thin air.

The other demon firing shots at me pauses. It's a pause I need and use to best effect. I turn my gaze on him and think the same thing. He too vanishes into thin air. I watch as the water fills in the place where his feet were a moment ago.

That leaves us with three.

I turn to the demon siphoning power from us, a nugget of hope forming in my chest. I point at him and bring down lightning. He raises a hand and absorbs the lightning. It's enough for him to stop siphoning the shield.

I feel another blast from Romora.

"Why isn't Disperao attacking?"

"It drains him to do what he's doing," Ikthiel says. "We have maybe a minute."

I swallow, my throat dry at the thought. If my shield fails, we're toast. We're all gone.

Bryce throws power at the siphoner, and I turn my gaze on Romora. I don't expect this to work. But maybe I can use my power to hurt her in some way.

So I think about the power inside of her. The power she wields and has wielded for millennia. I think about all the things she's done with it, all the lives she's taken and people she's hurt. And I find myself thinking the nastiest thoughts I'd had in years. I would take from her what she wants to take from me.

So I do.

I teleport her power out of her, summoning it across the beach from her body, like ashes rising from her skin.

She screams from the pain of it.

Disperao next to her looks furious. He looks at her and looks at me and forms an energy ball in his hands.

Romora, that demon notorious for millennia of terror, vanishes into thin air. Her power was her lifeline. I took her lifeline. I killed her.

The shield fails.

I look at Bryce. He's on his knees.

Then Disperao fires—

Ikthiel knocks me to the ground.

A blast of power so strong it reminds me of a sparkpoint, fills the air around us. Then it's gone, just like that, as if the flame were snuffed out.

"Fight it!" he screams.

I hear a voice cry out in pain and anguish. I don't know who cries out.

"Remember! Penny, you have to fight to remember!"

I look up at him. *What is he talking about?*

Lucy. He's talking about Lucy. How could I forget Lucy?

I push Ikthiel off me and look around us. Bryce is still on his knees, cradling his chest as if he might at any moment explode.

Disperao stands hunched over and drained. He's vulnerable. Where is Lucy?

Then it clicks.

Disperao's blast hit her. That's why Ikthiel wants me to remember. He wants me to know. She's gone.

A hole forms in my chest, a gaping feeling of pain I hadn't experienced in such a long time. Maybe not ever. Fury fills that hole. I climb to my feet and look at Disperao. He looks at me with fear.

I kill him with a blast that would take out a planet. I kill him so well I know even an immortal would not have survived the blast. He's gone. Destroyed and gone.

Ikthiel grabs me by the arms.

"She's gone," is all I can say. I'm in shock. I can feel it taking over my body.

"Hold it together," he says. "We have another problem."

What problem?

Bryce climbs to his feet, seemingly calm now.

Oh, right. Ikthiel lets me go. I face Bryce.

Bryce is a Witch.

He can't be, though. I would have sensed him.

Nothing makes sense. Bryce is a Witch. Lucy is gone. Reality shifts around me as rapidly and dangerously as that night on J'Phonk. I feel as though I can't get enough air in my lungs.

"I'm sorry," Bryce says, reaching for my hand.

"What?" I ask, recoiling from his touch. That's all I can think to say.

"I couldn't do it," he says. "I couldn't use it."

"Was that your sparkpoint?" I hiss.

"Penny—"

"*Was that your sparkpoint?*" I demand. Ikthiel grabs my arm.

"Penny," Bryce whispers. "No, I couldn't let it." His face folds in, crushed as he watches his words devastate me.

I pull my hand away from him, backing away from the contact. I can still feel Ikthiel's hand on my arm, and Lucy's loss is all the more real by his presence. But I can't focus on that. All I can see are Bryce's eyes as he looks at me. All I can see is the truth he's been hiding from me.

"Penny," he says again. He reaches for my hand again, but I

pull away further, recoiling from him, and take a step back.

"*Who are you?*" The question comes out in a hiss.

His outstretched hand closes to a fist, and he winces, his eyes squeezing shut as if to shut out the reality he is in. I know the feeling.

He turns away for a moment, his shoulders tense and set, steeling himself for what he is about to do. Then he turns back to me. Suddenly Ikthiel has both hands on me, his claws digging in. Ikthiel's reaction frightens me more than Bryce's face.

Then, Bryce lets the ax fall. "My name isn't Bryce Christopherson." He looks right at me as he says it. "My name is Boyce Reetur."

"*What?*" I hiss. Ikthiel's grip on me tightens, holding me back. "You're one of *them*?!"

Again, I am back on J'Phonk and again I am listening to the voices of Witches as they die. Like in all my nightmares, I feel the pain and the terror and the horror. And this boy who I trusted, liked even, he is one of *them*?

The betrayal hits me like a semi-truck, and I feel the pain going through every bone. A fragment of the younger Penny, the Penny who still had hope and kept it alive through all the anger, that fragment dies with the impact. My anger boils over.

"You *LIAR*. Your family kills Witches!" The words come out as a shout. I barely notice the flattening of the words. Ikthiel must have erected a sound wall to keep our conversation private. His arm is around my waist now, holding me back from Bryce or Boyce or whoever he is.

"I'm not like my family!" the boy I trusted says. "I didn't lie to you. I like you, and I was just trying to be your friend."

"I don't believe you! You lied to me!" I shout, pulling on Ikthiel's arm. "Let me *go*," I say to Ikthiel.

He shakes his head. "Hurting him will not help you," he whispers. Looking at his earnest face, I feel the tears starting.

"I trusted you," I say to the Reetur boy. "I trusted you, and you lied to me."

"Penny—"

"Don't say my name. I don't want you to speak to me again!" The tears warp my words.

I thought I was beyond hurt. My eyes go to where Lucy stood

on the beach not even a half hour ago. A sob begins to rise in my chest. Ikthiel wraps his arms around me, and I turn my face into his chest. I close my eyes, trying to block out the pain.

"Penny, *please*. I didn't want to hurt you," he says, his tone almost making me believe him. "My family—"

I turn my face back to him and say, "You are your family."

Even as I say it, the heat of power and betrayal in my voice, I'm not entirely sure it's true. But I am so angry and hurt that I don't care what I say. I don't care that his face is crushed by those words.

"Just go," I whisper. "Just leave."

For a moment, he seems to hesitate, reaches for me though I pull away and sink deeper into Ikthiel's embrace. A moment passes and I watch him turn and walk away. His footprints sink into the sand.

26

August 4

Penny

I bury my face in Ikthiel's chest again and let myself cry. I don't care if I'm showing him weakness. Too much pain has overloaded me now.

"It's ok," Ikthiel whispers in my ear. "I understand."

With his reassurance, I let myself feel the emotions taking me over. He picks me up and sits down again with me in his arms, holding me as I cry myself out. He holds me on the empty beach as I cry and cry for my lost friend—for my lost *friends*. I just let it out.

"I'm sorry," Ikthiel whispers. "I'm so sorry."

"He could have saved her," I whisper. "His sparkpoint could have saved her." I'm crying so hard the words come out warped.

"I know," Ikthiel says. "He's a Reetur. He chose his path. He'll have to live with it now."

I sniffle and lean back to look at him. "Will he become a demon?"

"Eventually," he whispers, "if it doesn't kill him first."

"Why didn't you let me kill him?" I demand, angry at Ikthiel now.

"You didn't really want to or you would have like you did with Waspira and Matchen," he says. "You have that power in you and you could have used it anyway. You chose not to."

Why would I choose to spare the boy who betrayed me? Who betrayed *us*?

"There must be some reason why," he whispers. Ikthiel pulls me closer, resting my head on his shoulder. His breath is in my ear as he says, "I'm sorry I couldn't save you both."

And just like that I crumble all over again. Ikthiel saved me like Bryce could have saved Lucy. Bryce could easily have saved us all. But he chose not to. Ikthiel chose to save me.

"I wish I could have spared you this pain," he says. And I believe him.

I'm not sure how much more time passes. "What do we do now?" I ask, a dead calm coming over me. I feel hollow and empty and cried out.

"We should find your mother and get you home," he says.

Oh, right. We're at the beach with my mother.

"Where did Bryce go?" I ask.

"He teleported."

Of course he did. Because of course he can.

Anger flares in me for just a nanosecond then goes away again. I'm tired of anger. I'm tired of grief. I'm tired of everything. I'm especially tired of Earth.

Ikthiel helps me up and holds my hand. "It's time I go back where I belong," I say. "It's time I get off this godforsaken planet."

He nods and doesn't argue.

We walk back down the beach. After a good fifteen or twenty minutes, we finally make it to my mother. She's standing next to the umbrella peering into the distance. She turns, sees us, and jogs up to us.

"What happened? You were gone so long," she says. "Where's Bryce?"

I shake my head. "We were attacked by some demons," I answer.

Her eyes go to Ikthiel and his hand in mine. "What?" she says, shock in her voice.

"They killed Lucy."

She looks confused. "Who's Lucy?"

A sob escapes my chest. "She was just here, you just talked to her."

She shakes her head. "I don't know what you're talking about," she says. "It was just us and Bryce today. I don't know any Lucy."

Ikthiel lets go of my hand and puts his arm around me. "It's Disperao. He erased her from spacetime. She no longer existed."

Sh—.

"There's nothing we can do?"

"No."

"I don't understand," my mother says. For a moment it looks like she wants to reach for me, but she doesn't. "What happened?"

"I had a friend named Lucy," I say softly, the past tense in my words taking little strips off my soul. "She's gone now. Erased from time. I remember her, but it's like she no longer exists." Then I remember her parents. They don't know she existed either, do they?

"No, they don't," Ikthiel answers my thoughts.

"The St. Johns don't know they had a daughter," I whisper.

"The St. Johns don't have a daughter," my mother says in confusion.

Again I can't control the tears or the sob. My emotions threaten to drown me. "I want to go home," is all I say. Not to that house where my mother lives. I want to go home to my room at the Academy. To the dwelling on Kaldreesa. To the places that no longer exist.

"I'll pack up," my mother says, interpreting my words wrongly. "Where's Bryce?" she asks again.

My face goes slack. I look her directly in the eye and say, "Bryce is a Witch. He's been hiding it from us all along."

My mother's jaw drops. She shakes her head. "He's *what?*" she asks.

"A Witch. Not just any Witch. He comes from a family of traitors," I add. I'm angry and I don't care who knows it.

She drops the towel she's holding. "Where is he?" she asks again.

"He teleported away. I'm sure he went home," I answer her. His whole family are Reeturs. A jolt of understanding runs through me. "His mother is a Witch. She's known about me all along."

"What?" my mother says again. "Thea Christopherson is a Witch?" She sounds incredulous. Like she can't quite believe what she's hearing. I just ignore her.

"We'll get you home," Ikthiel whispers to me.

I look up at him and can't even muster the energy to cover my pain. He puts a hand on my cheek, his claws even shorter than last time. I remember what Lucy asked me during our walk. I remember the question she asked that I didn't have an answer to. I think I know the answer.

"You do know the answer," he whispers.

My mother packs up everything and we head to the car. Ikthiel and I sit in the back seat, our fingers entwined and thumbs overlapping. I only feel pain and the comfort of his hand. The whole drive home that's all I focus on.

When we pull into the driveway, I get out and Ikthiel follows me. I head directly up to my bedroom. He shuts the door behind us. I sit down at my desk and open my laptop. I type out a message, pounding the keys in anger and grief.

To: Alicia Cole
(via Google Offworld Exchange)
From: Penelope Williams
Get me off this planet or I will leave of my own accord. Lucy is dead. I will find a place to go if you do not. I'm not asking.

I send the message. I don't care what she says, I'm going to leave as soon as I put everything in order and find a place to live.

Ikthiel sits perched on my bed. I turn around and face him in my chair.

"Will you come with me?" I ask. There is so much desperation in my voice. So much pain.

"I will come with you anywhere you want to go," he says softly. "You know that." He gives me a wry smile. "Even the shields of Widdershin couldn't hold me back."

My messages ping.

To: Penelope Williams
From: Alicia Cole
(via Google Offworld Exchange)
I don't know who Lucy is. I will make arrangements as soon as possible. Do not leave the planet till I tell you to.

F— her.

I'm not going to wait for someone else's *permission* to go where I want. I have friends and enough credits out there to live my whole life completely in space away from this awful place. No. I wasn't going to let someone like Alicia Cole dictate where I am allowed to live.

"When do you want to leave?" Ikthiel asks.

"Where can we go?"

"Anywhere you want," he says.

"Anywhere?" I ask.

He nods in answer. "I don't know where to go, but we'll make a life somewhere."

The prospect of never setting foot on Earth again feels tempting. I don't want to be here anymore. I didn't want to come back in the first place and if I hadn't Lucy would still be alive. The idea of making a life with Ikthiel feels like my last strand of hope.

"Yes." I can't see the future and right now I'm having trouble even imagining waking up tomorrow. But I know what I've known all along. I want Ikthiel here, permanently, by my side.

"When do you want to leave?" he asks again.

I shrug. "In a few days." I grimace. "I should tell my mother. She might flip out, but she needs to know."

The doorbell rings downstairs.

Ikthiel sits up straight in alarm. I look at him in confusion and open the door to my bedroom. He grabs my arm. I look up at him, startled.

"It's the Reeturs."

Fury fills me.

27

August 4

Penny

"You are not welcome here," I hear my mother say as I come down the stairs. Ikthiel is hot on my heels. He's not going to let me out of his sight after what happened at the beach.

Oh, *God*. Was the beach really only this morning? Only a couple hours ago? How can that be?

I step down the last stair and come around the corner to see my mother holding her own with the Reeturs. It's Bryce—or Boyce I guess—and his parents.

"There she is," his mother says.

His father pushes past my mother into our foyer and Bryce and his mother follow suit. His mother shuts the door behind them. Ikthiel shoves me behind him, his arm across my torso. I peer out from behind him and look the Reeturs in the eye.

"What do you want?" I growl. My mother's eyes widen as she stands on the other side of the Reeturs.

"Your power," Bryce's father says. "Why do you even align with them when you clearly align better with our side?"

"*Your side kills Witches*," I hiss. "You are responsible for so many deaths!" I practically shriek. "I was there on J'Phonk. I watched them die."

My mothers face goes pale with shock.

Bryce's father takes a step closer to me.

166

"Stay back," Ikthiel warns him. "Don't come any closer."

"Back down demon," he blusters. "This is between us and the Witch." He marches forward.

I don't even see Ikthiel move. I just see the claw marks across the Reeter's face. The father stumbles back, his wife catching him.

I just then realize Ikthiel's claws are long again. I guess he's feeling more his demonself at the moment. I don't care. I just know he's defending me. I want blood. I want to get rid of these Reeturs.

"Leave now," I warn them. "Before I do something you'll regret."

The mother grabs my mom. She cries out in shock. "I will kill her."

"Fine. Go ahead. She didn't try to save me," I say. "But if you do, I'll wipe you so far out of existence your whole family tree will feel the change." I pause and take a step forward. "Not only that, I will make it my personal mission to end every single Reeter, good or bad, in the whole of the universe. You *will* feel that!"

I watch Bryce's mother swallow. His father is bleeding on the tile floor. I'm annoyed by this so I flick a finger and the bleeding stops.

"Penny, *please*," Bryce says, barely above a whisper.

I turn on him. "*What do you want?*" I practically yell. "You, the traitor boy who hid who he was? Why? To get close to me?"

"No!" he shouts. "I really liked Lucy!"

"Not enough to save her," I accuse him. I'm shocked he even remembers her. But then again, in his sparkpoint is when the erasure happened. That might have been enough power to put him outside of time temporarily. Long enough that he would always remember. There is some consolation in that.

"I couldn't," he says. "You know that."

"No, I don't," I say, waving a finger at him. "You *chose* to let her die rather than save her with your sparkpoint. You *chose* this. You're just like them," I add, gesturing to his parents.

His face crumbles. That's the second time today I've destroyed him and it only took my words to do it. It's funny how I have so much power, but my words are what truly annihilate people.

"Enough!" his father shouts. He steps forward and grabs my wrist.

I immediately regret stopping his bleeding. But then I level my gaze at him and think to myself, *Let go.*

As if pried off by a set of pliers, his fingers lift stiffly. He fights it but only succeeds in falling to his knees in response. I level my power at him.

"No!" Bryce shouts. "Penny don't!"

"What's she doing?" his mother asks.

"She's going to vaporize him. She did it on the beach."

"I'll kill her," his mother snarls, choking my mother even more.

"No, you won't," I say, turning my gaze to her. I point one finger and she falls down like a sack of potatoes. My mother is intact.

Bryce goes to his mother and checks her pulse. I didn't kill her. Just forced her to sleep for a week. She would wake up tired too. I don't do things halfway anymore. Not since Lucy . . . I swallow to keep from choking up.

"Penelope," Ikthiel whispers. "Let them go."

I turn to him, fire in my veins at the mere suggestion. "*Why?*" I demand to know.

"Because of what I can see."

And I pry into his mind to see Bryce and me standing side by side with Altair and Ikthiel on some rocky landscape somewhere presumably far away. If Ikthiel sees him, then it must be true.

"No," I whisper.

"Yes," he says. "He'll be needed. Let them go."

"What about his parents?" I ask.

"Them too," he says softly. "You're not a murderer. You defended yourself on the beach. You took the lives of demons. You are not a murderer." He takes my hand. I can feel myself softening, the anger subsiding to the throbbing pain of grief. "You are better than they are."

Bryce's father climbs to his feet.

I turn back to them. "Take her and your traitorous son with you," I command. "If I ever see you again, I will make good on my threat and destroy you all."

"Even *you* don't have that kind of power," he spits the words out at me.

"Watch me," I answer softly. "Now go before I change my mind."

Bryce's father picks up his mother. Bryce opens the door and lets them through. He looks back at me once, a look of longing and sadness on his face. He knows what he did was wrong. He knows he was as bad to me as I was to Lucy, worse perhaps because of the magnitude of his betrayal. He shuts the door behind him. I sincerely hope I never see him again. Ikthiel's vision makes that unlikely.

Silence reigns as I stare at my mother and Ikthiel's hand holds onto my arm. The blood on the floor is the only reminder that the incident transpired. I'm angry and deflated. I feel like I could have done more, but that's just the anger talking. I know logically Ikthiel is right, that I would have regretted killing the Reeturs. I just wish he wasn't right.

The ugly truth is I don't want to be a nice person anymore. I feel it in my bones in that moment. I feel how much the pain and the trauma and the terror have changed me. How much I've changed on this one day. I feel the tendrils of malevolence seeping into me, trying to turn me into something else.

"Penny, you saw them kill people?" my mother gasps out. She is still leaning against the door, still clearly in shock.

I tear my gaze away from the blood on the floor. I meet my mother's gaze. "They killed every Witch on J'Phonk except for six. Those six escaped with me and Ikthiel and Altair."

"Dear God," she mutters. "The Christopherson's had something to do with that?"

"They're allied with the people who are responsible," I answer. "And clearly they want my power, or else they wouldn't have come here."

"What are you going to do?" she asks me.

I exchange a look with Ikthiel. This is the moment. "I'm going to leave Earth," I answer. "I'm going to go back out there and fight the war with the Kolvat and try to solve this problem we have."

"What problem?"

I smile wryly. "Oh, just a creature from beyond the universe eating reality," I answer nonchalantly.

She barks out a laugh. I think she's in shock. "'Oh just' . . ."

Definitely in shock.

"Mom, you should sit down," I say.

Ikthiel lets go of me and I go to her. I lead her into the kitchen and make her sit on a stool. I pour a few glasses of water from a pitcher and hand her one. "Drink," I say.

She stares up at me and then takes a sip of the water. I hand one of the glasses to Ikthiel because he needs it too. Then I take the third for myself.

It's been a long day.

"You're leaving?" she says again.

"Yes," I answer. "In a few days probably. I can't stay here. Not after everything that happened today." There is pain in my voice as I say it. Or as I avoid saying it. I set my glass down not wanting to drop it. Ikthiel sets his down too and comes up to me. He puts an arm around me and holds me close. I don't know how long we stay like that, but I hear the clink of the glass as my mother sets hers on the counter. I pull away from him.

"Are you going with her?" she asks Ikthiel.

"Yes," he says. "Of course."

My mother studies Ikthiel for a moment. It's like she's seeing him for the first time. Her gaze goes to his hands and her brow knits. "You're a demon?" she asks.

"Can you see my claws?" he asks.

She nods.

"How?" I ask.

"Knowledge breakthrough," he answers. "If you know—really *know*—about demons, then you can see through the shield."

"Isn't that dangerous?" I ask.

He merely shrugs.

"Can you promise me you'll keep her safe?" my mother says suddenly.

I shake my head as if to clear it. "You care about that?" I ask bluntly. I don't have the patience to care about anyone's feelings right now.

"Yes," she answers earnestly. "I do care." It's as if she's realizing it herself. "Are you coming back?"

"Probably not," I answer. "At least, not till I'm done."

She looks up at me. She's still sitting in that stool and from this angle she looks small and frightened. I know she feels that way. I don't know what she's thinking right now, but I do know she's frightened.

"Will you be safe out there?"

"No," I answer. "I'm never safe anywhere anymore. I just have to deal with it."

I watch her watch me. I don't know what to make of her questions or her answers. I don't feel like prying into her thoughts because, if I'm totally honest, I'm not sure I care.

"Will you tell me if you're coming back?" she asks.

I think for a moment. "I'll leave you a way to communicate with me," I answer. "My email will still work, for example."

She gets up from the stool. She approaches me and pulls me into a hug in a way she hasn't in almost six years. I let her hug me and even hug her back. I don't know what she needs in that moment, but clearly this is part of it. She pulls back from me, puts hand on each shoulder.

"I wish I had known all those years ago what you would go through, what you would become," she says. "There is a lot I would have done differently, a lot I would have prevented. I wish I would have known." And that's all she says. No apology. It would be ridiculous to say I'm sorry at this point. It would be so pale in comparison to the years of abuse and trauma I had gone through.

"I'm going to pack," I say, thinking of the few things I actually care about taking with me. "I'm going to leave on Monday."

She pulls away and takes our glasses to the sink. Then she turns around and says, "Alright. If you're leaving, then be careful. And you," she adds, pointing at Ikthiel, "watch out for her."

Ikthiel straightens up and looks at her. I don't think he's been dressed down by a mother in probably a hundred years. He nods his head soberly and doesn't argue. I know he was already planning to look out for me anyway. This is not a task he would turn down.

"Just be careful," she says to me. It's sincere as far as I can tell.

She goes back to washing the dishes and I head upstairs. Ikthiel follows me.

Once in my bedroom with the door shut, he pulls me into a hug and whispers, "I'm so sorry."

I shake my head against his chest. I feel so much older than I am. I feel ancient by human standards.

"You've been through a lot," he whispers. "It's only fair you feel that way."

"I just wanted to be normal," I grumble.

"Well, even without power, you were never going to be that," he teases. He kisses the top of my head and lets me go.

I go to my closet and pull my Academy bag out from the back. I begin packing.

My email goes off on my computer. I check the message.

To: Penelope Williams
From: Alicia Cole
(via Google Offworld Exchange)
Relocation approved. Await instructions prior to departing Earth.

It better be approved.

Yeah, like I am going to wait.

But that makes it final. We're leaving Earth. I honestly don't know if I'll ever return.

28

August 8

Penny

The day of my departure came faster than I expected. I pack up the last of my things and clean up the rest of my room, putting everything carefully in its place. My mother has said she would leave it undisturbed, but I don't know how long that will last when I'm gone for years. Still. I should at least have everything where it belongs.

Ikthiel is coming to fetch me in a few minutes. I'm just looking around my room one last time, taking in the trappings of my time here. I only spent about a year in this room. It never really felt like home. My cramped room on Widdershin was the closest thing to a home I've ever had. Now I don't have that. But maybe, just maybe, I could find something like that again.

I pick up my backpack and my Academy bag and head downstairs. I find my mother waiting in the kitchen downing what is probably her third cup of coffee. She's been nervous since I announced my departure. I don't really know how to deal with it. I don't know if anything will ever be fixed between us. And I'm not sure I care enough to want it to be. She's finally making a tiny effort in the eleventh hour. I don't know if it'll be enough.

"You're packed?" she says, setting down her coffee cup.

"Yeah," I say, dropping my bags near the dining table. "Ikthiel will be here soon."

"What about the other friend, Altair?"

I shrug. "He's busy doing something, I don't know what," I say. In truth he had barely responded to what I sent him. He had acknowledged that I was leaving Earth and that he looked forward to seeing me. But he hadn't added any details. I honestly don't know what's going on with him and where he is.

"Where will you go?" she asks me.

"I don't know," I answer truthfully. "Ikthiel is taking me to the nearest Witches' Station. From there, I don't know." I shrug. "We'll find something. Some work to do, some lead about the Weapons."

"The Hammer?" she asks, clearly remembering.

"Yes," I answer. "And any others we might discover."

"Do you need anything to eat?" she asks.

"No," I answer. "We'll eat when we get there. I miss the food."

Silence falls over us. I don't know what to say at this point. She picks up her coffee cup again and takes a drink. Then she seems to remember something.

"You said you'd leave an email?" she asks.

"Oh, right," I say. I had forgotten. And I honestly wasn't sure I wanted her to use it. I take the notepad from beside the fridge and pick up a pencil. The grocery list is on the first page. I pull a sheet from the back and scribble down my Google Offworld Exchange email address. It'll ping my wrist communicator with any new emails from Earth.

"Here you go," I say, handing her the paper. "It'll reach me anywhere."

"Thank you," she says, taking the paper. She sets it on the counter next to her.

A pop signals Ikthiel's arrival in the living room. He walks through the house and comes to us in the kitchen. He comes to me and gives me an awkward side-hug. I return the side-hug.

"You ready?" he asks.

"Yes," I answer. I go to my two bags and shoulder my backpack. He picks up my Academy bag.

"Is this everything?" he asks.

I nod. I walk up to my mother and give her an awkward hug. I don't know why I do it. Maybe she doesn't deserve forgiveness from me. Maybe she is as horrible as I think she could be. I don't know. I just know that now that I'm leaving I don't want the skeletons from my past chasing me across the universe.

"I'll be careful," I say, before she can say it.

She nods. There's nothing else to be said. She just watches as I go to stand by Ikthiel.

He wraps his arm around me, pulling me close to him, and we pop out of the kitchen.

An instant later, we rematerialize on a space station. We walk out of the block of transit squares and down a promenade, hand in hand as we go. Ikthiel leads us to what can only be a bar—bars are recognizable everywhere. We're directed to a cozy table at the back, one of the booths set up for humanoids. He sets my bag next to us and we cozy up together on the seat.

"I'm proud of you," he says suddenly.

"Why?" I ask.

"Because of how you handled your mother," he says. "And because of . . . well . . . everything."

I give him a crooked smile. "I'm proud of you too," I say.

He runs a hand through my ponytail, a gesture that feels intimate and loving. I study his dark eyes and his whole expression. He's a demon but he's the only person I trust in the whole universe. The only person I trust fully, anyway. I haven't quite articulated my feelings for this person. Not yet.

"You know the truth," he whispers.

A waitress comes over to us and takes our order. Ikthiel orders food that won't poison us and she leaves again. Ikthiel pulls me closer to him, our hips touching and my body leaning into his.

"The truth?" I whisper back.

"About how you feel," he says.

"I don't know your truth," I answer tartly. "And until I do, well, I won't say anything."

His mouth twitches in amusement. "You know how I feel." He pauses. "Do I need to spell it out?"

"Are we ready for that?" I ask wryly.

His gaze leaves mine and I watch as he surveys the bar. "I don't know," he admits, looking back at me. "Are you?"

"I don't know," I answer. "I'm not sure anyway." After a pause, I add, "I want to be."

"Out here, things are different," he says.

I follow his gaze across the bar, at the aliens all socializing and drinking or eating. I watch creatures so vastly different from me that I can't comprehend their differences. But I feel better here. I feel safer somehow. Like this is where I belong.

Maybe I do.

Ikthiel looks back at me. "I care about you," he begins. I know this part. "I would do anything to protect you." Still stuff I know. "And I . . . feel things for you I haven't felt in a hundred years."

"Am I safe with you?" I ask him. I know the answer, but I need to hear it.

"Always."

"Then I would say I feel for you what you feel for me," I answer. It's as far as I'm willing to go at this time. He's saved me so many times at this point. I trust him with my life. But I'm not ready yet. I know that for certain.

He kisses my forehead softly. He doesn't say anything else.

He doesn't have to.

I've lost so much over the past week. I've lost so much of myself in the losing. I don't know how to keep from falling apart. I don't know how to be myself again. But with Ikthiel, I feel like it's possible. I feel like I *could* be myself again. The version of myself that saw his claws for what they were. Or a new version of myself that knows him and loves him. Maybe that's the key. You don't go backwards to what you once were. You move forward to what you are now and transform into what you could become.

Our food comes. I set aside my thoughts and my anger and my grief. I set aside the fact that Lucy is gone, and my soul is weary. I even set aside the conundrum of the Universe-Eater and everything that could be at stake. Right here, right now, I just live in the moment. I try to let go and be here with Ikthiel in this bar. I stare at my food, unable to take a bite.

Ikthiel takes my hand and I look up at him. "I'm sorry for everything that's happened," he says. "I wish I could erase all your pain."

I just watch him.

Then he says, "I've lived a long life and I've never known the true meaning of the word. But with you I know what it means. I know the act of love." My stomach is in my throat, I have so many butterflies. "You might not be ready to say it, but I am. After this past week and almost losing you again, I'm ready." So he kisses me, just once. Just a soft touch of our lips. "I love you, Penelope."

The corners of my mouth turn up. I can't help it. It feels light and airy to feel that way. To have those feelings given to me. I don't know if I can say it yet. But I feel it. I *know* I feel it.

He turns back to his food. I turn back to mine.

We carry on as if nothing happened.

EPILOGUE

Alicia Cole watches the Hammer in action. The empty field on this barren planet is littered with too many pockmarked spots where the Hammer's energy has flamed out. No one who can hold the damn thing can seem to wield it. It feels like they're at a dead end.

"We need to find the person who originally wielded it," Clathlor says. "Or just have the Powerhouse wield it."

She gives him a sour expression that translates even though he is Telusian and doesn't know human expressions. "I highly doubt that's a good idea," she says.

"It may be our only choice," he answers. "It may be the only thing we can do."

"And what happens if we let the Powerhouse wield the Hammer and it does *nothing* to stop the Kolvat?" she argues. "I don't think it's a good idea to just throw that power around without knowing for certain."

"I think you're making a mistake," he says. "I think the only way we're going to win this war is to throw everything we can at it."

"Come back in," Alicia Cole calls to the three Witches working in the middle of the field. The Granician, the Ingtax, and the Glorandyne all move in their direction, the Ingtax carrying the Hammer. When they get back, Alicia Cole reaches for the Hammer again, and once again it refuses her. It feels personal.

"That's because it is personal," a voice calls out. Five species all follow the sound of the voice. A figure walks towards them, a humanoid with a long black braid and dark eyes. As she approaches, the Hammer brightens to a blue-white glow. She reaches for it and it leaps from the Ingtax's appendage to her hand.

"Who are you?" Alicia Cole demands.

"Naymeth Nireson," she says, as if that explains everything.

"Like the mythological figure?" the Granician asks in their stony voice.

"The same," she answers. She hefts the Hammer. The light brightens to blinding and power strikes a nearby boulder. "Where is the person who retrieved it? She's the one who should be wielding it."

"What did I say?" Clathlor says to Alicia Cole.

She looks rueful, angry almost. She can't stand the Powerhouse. There's something so cocky and annoying about her. And her association with the demon is unnerving. It's worrisome. What if she becomes like the Reeturs? Then they would have the most powerful Witch of all time fighting for the wrong side. This is why she needs to be controlled.

"I still disagree," she says. "And I will veto any decision that puts the power in her hands."

"Then you will fail," Naymeth Nireson says. "You will fail due to your own arrogance." The words are harsh.

Alicia Cole scoffs. "We have resources we can deploy."

"Never in the millennia I have lived have I seen the kind of power that the wielder can display," Naymeth Nireson retorts. "I was there at the beginning. I placed the Mallet to be found. I laid the spell down. She is the worthy one. She can wield it. And if you know what's good for you and this universe, she *will* wield it."

"No," Alicia Cole says coldly. "I don't know who you are. I will not bend to the will of a complete stranger."

"Then you will forfeit the whole universe."

"Alicia, listen to her," the Granician says. "She knows what she's talking about."

Alicia Cole turns on the Granician. "How do we know she's not some agent of the other side?"

"Because she's the Hero of Abergast," the Ingtax says. "The Prophet of the Toruls."

"She's lived a thousand thousand lives," the Granician adds.

"She would know."

Naymeth Nireson hands the Hammer back to the Ingtax. "Thank you for indulging me," she says. "Let her wield it or you are all dead."

And just like that Naymeth Nireson walks away from five stunned Witches. Alicia Cole lets her anger simmer. She would not be bullied into handing the Hammer over to a *child*.

"We have no choice."

"We *always* have a choice," Alicia Cole says.

"And we're making the wrong one."

"We shall see," she says. She walks away from the four.

Clathlor shaking his head. "We have no hope to beat them."

"Then we'll have to find a way to get the Hammer into her hands," the Ingtax says, studying the Weapon.

"That we will."

ABOUT THE AUTHOR

Olivia "Lollie" Jones Black has been writing in some form or other since she was eleven. A background in science provides inspiration for her work. Her writing blends both science fiction and fantasy, epic and mundane, and leans on her science education to incorporate science fact into science fiction.

A cat who thinks she owns the computer occasionally helps with the writing. She lives on the east coast.

www.ingramcontent.com/pod-product-compliance
Lightning Source LLC
Chambersburg PA
CBHW031445200726
48289CB00007BB/2423